The
Hauntings of
Williamsburg, Yorktown,
and Jamestown

John F. Blair, Publisher
Winston-Salem,
North Carolina

The Hauntings of Williamsburg, Yorktown, and Jamestown

Jackie Eileen Behrend

DESIGN BY DEBRA LONG HAMPTON
PRINTED AND BOUND BY
EDWARDS BROTHERS, INC.
PHOTOGRAPHS BY THE AUTHOR

Second Printing, 2000

Front cover photographs and photographs on pages iii and ix are of the
Amblers' colonial mansion in Jamestown.

*The paper in this book meets the guidelines for permanence and durability of the
Committee on Production Guidelines for Book Longevity of the Council on
Library Resources.*

Library of Congress Cataloging-in-Publication Data

Behrend, Jackie Eileen, 1957–
    The hauntings of Williamsburg, Yorktown, and Jamestown / Jackie
Eileen Behrend.
        p.   cm.
    Includes index.
    ISBN 0-89587-210-2 (alk. paper)
    1. Williamsburg (Va.)—History—Anecdotes. 2. Yorktown (Va.)—
History—Anecdotes. 3. Jamestown (Va.)—History—Anecdotes. 4.
Ghosts—Virginia—Williamsburg—Anecdotes. 5. Ghosts—Virginia—
Yorktown—Anecdotes. 6. Ghosts—Virginia—Jamestown—Anecdotes.
I. Title.
F234.W7B436 1998
975.5'42—dc21   98–2973

The book is dedicated to the
one person I can always count on,
my best friend and mother,
Marlene.

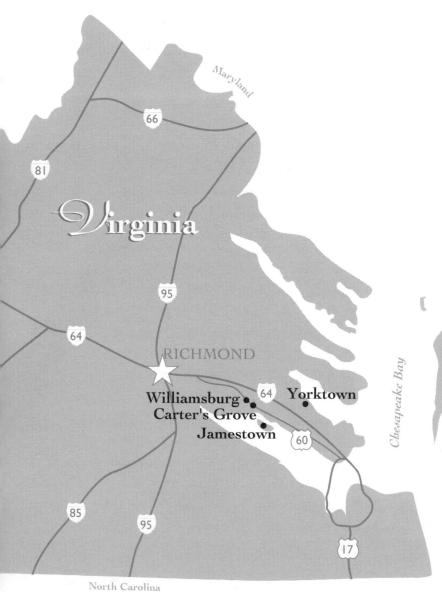

Table of Contents

Introduction   ix

Williamsburg

Yorktown

Jamestown

Carter's Grove

Introduction

Virginia's historic triangle, encompassing Williamsburg, Yorktown, and Jamestown, is the perfect example of a region that preserves its past while moving into the future. Few parts of the country can boast that they have been involved in so many momentous events over the course of such a long period of time. Perhaps that explains why there have been so many stories from this area about strange occurrences during the last several centuries.

According to parapsychologists, spirits that have been dormant for centuries can be awakened by a flurry of activity and sounds. In the 1920s and 1930s, a major restoration project found the village of Williamsburg undergoing complete re-creation. In recent years, Yorktown has also undergone extensive renovations, and excavations continue on the Jamestown site even today. It is possible that the constant pounding of hammers and the digging by archaeologists may have jolted some of these spirits from their sleep. *The Hauntings of Williamsburg, Yorktown, and Jamestown* gives the reader a glimpse at some of the secrets and mysteries that these slumbering ghosts have revealed.

The ghostly tales featured in this book come from a variety of sources. A few of these spooky sagas have been passed down orally from generation to generation. Some were found in musty old diaries or historical documents. I discovered many of these tales while conducting personal interviews and researching archives to find stories that I could incorporate in my "Haunted Williamsburg" walking tours. I have even included a few personal encounters with spirits when they seemed appropriate.

Some of these hauntings were first reported centuries ago. Other sightings may have occurred only recently. For example, Sharon Daily, a visitor from Harrisburg, Pennsylvania, recently told me that she had concrete evidence that spirits really do exist in Williamsburg. She showed me a photograph that she took in front of Bruton Parish Church. In the picture were the figures of four people—two men and two women—dressed in nineteenth-century clothing. Their images seemed to jump off the paper, as if they were three dimensional. These figures appear to be apparitions because you can see the background through their silhouettes.

Throughout this book, you will notice that each spirit seems to have a different reason for haunting a particular place. Some people believe that spirits remain tied to the earth because of unfinished business or their need to try to right injustices. Some believe that an event can be so traumatic that the spirit stays locked in the time when that event occurred. The latter may explain the stories in this book about the ghosts of soldiers who died fighting for freedom during the Revolutionary War or who lost their lives in the Battle of Williamsburg during the Civil War.

The background for each of these stories has been researched, and every attempt has been made to make the tales historically accurate. I have also tried to insure that each account is corroborated by witnesses or by evidence found in written documents.

It is also important to remember that this book was written for enjoyment. This book was not intended to be a vehicle to convince someone of the presence of the supernatural.

Hopefully, this book will show that Virginia's "haunted" triangle is not only a place of history, but one of mystery as well. After reading this book, you may realize that the region holds onto its memories—and its unearthly specters. There appear to be many lost souls lurking on the tranquil, darkened streets of this region. While reading *The Hauntings of Williamsburg, Yorktown, and Jamestown*, you may be surprised to discover just how much "spirit" this magnificent area really has. Whether or not you believe in ghosts, I hope you enjoy these fascinating tales.

Williamsburg

While touring the picturesque streets of Williamsburg, it may be hard to imagine the town's humble beginnings. In 1699, Virginia's general assembly decided to move the colony's capital from Jamestown to Middle Plantation. Middle Plantation was an outpost located near the six-mile wall that was built to protect the peninsula from invading Indians. After the capital was moved to Middle Plantation, the new capital was renamed Williamsburg in honor of the King of England, William III.

Although the modest homes that were built in Williamsburg's early years were a far cry from the wealthy homes that you see restored in today's Colonial Williamsburg, the settlement was prosperous even in its early stages.

The General Court met in Williamsburg each year in April and October for a two-week period, and the Court of Oyer and Terminer met there in June and December. These two courts met in Williamsburg for periods called "public times." During public times, leaders such as Thomas Jefferson and Patrick Henry, who argued cases before the General Court, could be seen strolling on Duke of Gloucester Street.

Crowds would gather in the Capitol Building to listen to the eloquent speeches made by the members of the assembly. As the rhetoric just prior to the Revolutionary War heated up, the crowds grew.

During public times, vendors poured into Williamsburg to

sell their crafts and products. The members of Williamsburg's society gave grand balls and parties. Everyone wore their finest clothing, even if it was only to parade through the streets of town. Taverns and lodging houses teemed with burgesses and other travelers who filled the city during the legislative sessions. Williamsburg was an exciting, prosperous, and happy place to be, in spite of the mounting tensions with England.

Once the Revolutionary War broke out, the atmosphere in Williamsburg changed. Politicians who sided with England were forced to resign their positions. Some citizens left town and fled to England for their safety. Some prominent families were torn apart forever because of dissension over whether the colonies should have their independence.

As if all of this turmoil were not enough, the general assembly decided to move Virginia's capital to Richmond in 1780. At that point, property values decreased, and the town's population declined.

In June 1781, Lord Cornwallis's English troops invaded Williamsburg and declared martial law. A 1775 proclamation by the colonial governor of Williamsburg offered freedom to slaves and indentured servants who belonged to Patriots, if they ran away to join the English army. As slaves took advantage of this offer, citizens began to panic. Cornwallis and his men burned homes, looted stores, and took whatever they wanted. For several days, there was a reign of terror in Williamsburg. Although the townspeople knew American troops were in Virginia, they had no way of knowing that the impending confrontation at Yorktown would decide the war.

Cornwallis's troops pulled out of Williamsburg on July 4, and Lafayette and his troops entered the town soon after. In October, the Battle of Yorktown effectively ended the era of British rule. Although the war was over, Williamsburg witnessed the horrors of battle as wounded soldiers flooded the town. Private homes, public buildings, and the campus of the College of William and Mary were all turned into makeshift hospitals.

As the memories of the Revolutionary War faded, Williamsburg became a quiet, tranquil town. A person could walk half the length of the once-bustling Duke of Gloucester Street without seeing another human being. Cows, chickens, and goats roamed freely on the dusty roads. This peaceful setting ended when Williamsburg once again became the setting for military involvement—this time during the Civil War.

By the turn of the century, the city had become a sleepy, run-down township. Despite the decline in Williamsburg's status, there were eighty-eight original eighteenth- and early nineteenth-century buildings still standing when Reverend W.A.R. Goodwin came to Williamsburg as rector of Bruton Parish Church in 1903. It was the existence of this group of historic structures that gave Goodwin the inspiration to restore the village.

In 1926, Reverend Goodwin, with financial backing from John D. Rockefeller, Jr., began the restoration of the colonial capital. A restoration project of this magnitude had never been attempted in this country, but it was a triumphant success. After decades of intense planning and meticulous reconstruction,

Williamsburg regained its eighteenth-century grandeur.

Today, Williamsburg stands as a testament to the colonial period. Over 3 million people visit Colonial Williamsburg annually. If you visit Colonial Williamsburg, there are several ways you can tour the village. The historic streets are open to the public. To tour the buildings, an admission ticket is usually needed.

The Wagon of Death

During the eighteenth century,
the Wagon of Death traveled down Nicholson Street.

SINCE WILLIAMSBURG was the capital of Virginia during most of the eighteenth century, any free person accused of a felony had to be tried in this city. During this period, there was little compromise in the judicial process. If a person was convicted of murder, arson, horse stealing, forgery, or piracy, he was often sentenced to hang. As a result, Williamsburg was the scene of numerous hangings.

If a person was sentenced to hang, it was thought that keeping him confined for a prolonged period of time was inhumane and cruel. Hanging was regarded a kinder punishment than imprisonment.

In the eighteenth century, this may have been the case. The conditions the inmates had to endure during their imprisonment were horrible. The cells were small, cramped, and unheated. The tiny barred windows contained no glass to protect the prisoners from the elements.

Prisoners slept on piles of insect-ridden straw. During later excavations of the prison grounds, heavy shackles were unearthed, providing evidence that prisoners were often chained to the floor.

Lice covered the walls. Roaches and rodents scurried throughout the cells. The smell alone was almost unbearable. Considering these conditions, death may have seemed a better option.

If found guilty of a heinous crime, the criminal was held in the overcrowded jail until the "Wagon of Death" came to escort him to the gallows. Long before this death wagon was in view, the condemned man could hear the creaking of the cart's wheels as it rolled down Nicholson Street. The prisoner was then forced to sit on his own coffin for the mile-long ride to Hangman's Road, knowing full well he would be inside the casket on the way back.

When the prisoner arrived at the gallows, he was usually the center of a social event. A public hanging brought people to the capital from all over the surrounding countryside. It was usually a festive, cheering crowd that greeted the prisoner when he arrived in the Wagon of Death.

A person can't help but feel a little sorry for the wayward criminals of the eighteenth century. We can only imagine the terror and panic they must have felt as they rode on the Wagon of Death, watching their last few minutes of life tick away.

The days of the hangman's rope are long gone. No physical evidence remains of the hangman's gallows on the outskirts of Williamsburg, but you can still visit the original Public Gaol, as it was called then.

This jail is one of the oldest buildings in the former capital city. It housed murderers, pirates, marauding Indians, runaway slaves, and common debtors until 1780, when Virginia's capital moved to Richmond. It continued to house offenders until 1910.

In addition to the jail, there have been other less tangible reminders of how we used to treat our criminals. For well over a century, haunting stories of the Wagon of Death have been reported. People living on Nicholson Street speak of hearing the sounds of a horse and wagon in the predawn hours. They dash to their windows, but they see nothing of this mysterious carriage or its ill-fated passengers.

James Daughtery, a guest at the spacious Coke-Garrett House in June 1985, told of an inexplicable incident he experienced early one morning while sleeping in one of the rooms facing Nicholson Street. He said, "I awoke to the sound of horses and the cracking of a whip. A loud gruff voice commanded the animals to move faster. I thought it was far too early for Colonial Williamsburg to have their horses on the street, but I knew I wasn't imagining what I was hearing. Then I remembered the myth of the Wagon of Death. I was determined to see if it really did exist. I ran to the window, but the street was empty of both horses and people. I was disappointed that I didn't see the death wagon for myself, but at least I knew I'd heard it."

Early one foggy morning in April 1992, Donald Reeves, a Colonial Williamsburg employee, had a similar experience. He was working in the Carpenter's Yard, then on Nicholson Street, preparing for a busy day of visitors. Donald said, "I was setting up the tool display in the shed when I heard the clacking of horses' hooves and the creaking of wagon wheels. I didn't think much of it until I realized it was so early, the sun hadn't risen yet. I still didn't pay much attention until I heard the sound of a whip cracking. Being an animal lover, I was upset thinking the horses were being mistreated. I ran outside but there wasn't anything there."

It would seem those living and working on Nicholson Street are not alone in their experiences. Tourists staying on Hangman's Road (now Capitol Landing Road) have heard the illusive horse and wagon as well. Kitty Miller was sleeping in a nearby hotel when she, too, was awakened by strange noises. Kitty is certain she heard, "a horse whinny and the sound of a crowd cheering. I thought some event of Colonial Williamsburg's was going on outside. I couldn't believe they would be doing this so early in the morning, while people were trying to sleep. I was angry because I didn't sleep well the night before and I needed to get some rest. I went to the window to see what was going on, but the yard was empty! The sounds of the crowd just faded away."

To this day, no one has actually seen the legendary Wagon

of Death or the horses that pull it. Most will agree, however, it not only exists, but continues to pass down the historic streets of Williamsburg, as it has done for almost three centuries.

The Public Gaol is located on the eastern end of Nicholson Street in Colonial Williamsburg. Nicholson Street runs parallel to Duke of Gloucester Street, which is the principal road in the historic area. Look for the Capitol Building at the very end of Duke of Gloucester Street. The jail is to the left (northern) side of the capitol. Tours are given from 9:30 a.m. until 5:30 p.m. A pass is needed to tour the building. Call (757) 220-7645 for additional information.

Loony Lucy Ludwell

The Ludwell-Paradise House

AFTER VIRGINIA'S CAPITAL was moved to Richmond in 1780, Williamsburg went through its sleepy years. However, there was one local woman, Lucy Ludwell, who added color to this otherwise drab time for the town. The townspeople thought Lucy was "eccentric," but no one could say she didn't keep things interesting.

Lucy was a member of one of Williamsburg's prominent families. Her grandfather was a member of the House of Burgesses and one of the city's original trustees. Her father, Philip Ludwell III, was a member of the governor's council. Around 1755, Ludwell built a large two-story, red-brick mansion that is now called the Ludwell-Paradise House. When Lucy's father died, she inherited the house.

Although Lucy's family was well respected in Williamsburg,

Lucy never endeared herself to the townspeople. Lucy Ludwell was not considered a kind, or even a particularly nice person. When she met and married John Paradise on one of her many visits to England, the townspeople were not unhappy to hear that the couple planned to settle in London. Lucy decided to rent her Williamsburg home while she lived abroad.

In London, the couple became part of a socially elite crowd of artists and writers. After the Revolutionary War broke out, the newly created state of Virginia confiscated Lucy's house.

When John died in 1795, Lucy was alone and penniless. Like it or not, she was forced to return to Williamsburg. It took her several years to regain ownership of her property and get permission to return to Virginia, but she was finally allowed to return to Williamsburg in 1805. By the time she returned to her home, Lucy had picked up a few unusual habits along the way.

In her deluded mind, Lucy thought of herself as royalty. Therefore, it was only fitting that the people of Williamsburg treat her as such. Lucy soon adopted the strange practice of parading up and down Duke of Gloucester Street, giving the royal wave, while her servant followed behind, holding the bottom of her skirt. She would keep up this odd behavior for hours on end.

As time passed, Lucy added another detail to this bizarre act. She would sneak into her neighbors' homes and take their clothing. She would then go to the Ludwell-Paradise House and dress herself with two or three dresses and two or three hats before resuming her queenly walks.

By this time, the townspeople were becoming quite alarmed. The last straw finally came when Lucy began taking make-believe carriage rides in her stable. She invited her neighbors to join her for these peculiar events. Since Lucy was a large, intimidating woman, it was easy for her to coax leery neighbors into agreeing. She then had her slaves push and rock the horseless coach while she pointed out the sights of London. Sadly, Lucy truly believed she was showing her captive audience the skyline of her favorite city!

That was it for poor Lucy. By 1816, the townspeople got together and had her committed to the Public Hospital, a mental institution on Francis Street.

To say the least, Lucy Ludwell did not go willingly. She dug her heels into the ground as several men tried to escort her to her new destination. It took a group of five to carry her the half-mile to the asylum. As they attempted to cart her away, Lucy made quite a spectacle of herself. Screaming and shouting at the top of her lungs, she vowed she would return to her home one day. Ironically, the same home she was so anxious to leave for London was now looking quite good. Within two years of her incarceration, Lucy went completely insane and died in the asylum.

The fine home Lucy fought so desperately not to leave changed hands several times before it was finally purchased by John D. Rockefeller, Jr., in 1926 for a mere eight thousand dollars.

For quite some time no one knew if Lucy had kept her vow to return to the Ludwell-Paradise House. The beautiful mansion had fallen into great disrepair. Five years after Colonial Williamsburg purchased the building, restoration began. Soon after restoration began, workers started to talk of strange happenings going on inside the old colonial home.

A letter written by one of these laborers, Walter Whipples, was found in the archives. It tells an extraordinary story. Whipples wrote, "Tools are missing when we arrive in the morning, and our papers are thrown about as if someone had a temper tantrum. Many documents needed to renovate the building cannot be found at all. Also, the water turns on and off by itself, and pounding noises can be heard coming from empty rooms. Sometimes, I'm actually afraid to go to work! It is obvious we are unwelcome intruders. I truly cannot wait until this project is completed."

Needless to say, the fearful Mr. Whipples was convinced Lucy had kept her promise to come back to the Ludwell-Paradise House. Because she had to die to be able to come home, it appears her spirit now refuses to leave the house.

The Ludwell-Paradise House is situated midway along the mile-long Duke of Gloucester Street between Queen and Colonial Streets in Colonial Williamsburg. Most of the buildings in the historic district have identification signs on them. This house is next to the Prentis Store.

Evil Stalks the Peyton Randolph House

The Peyton Randolph House

PEYTON RANDOLPH was one of the most influential men in eighteenth-century Virginia. Descended from an illustrious family, he counted Pocahontas, John Rolfe, and Powhatan among his ancestors. His father, John Randolph, was the first Virginian to be granted knighthood. He was knighted for his diligent work on behalf of the Crown.

Ironically, Peyton became one of the strongest supporters of the Patriots' quest for independence from England. In 1766, Peyton was elected Speaker of the House of Burgesses, and in 1774, he was elected the first president of the Continental

Congress. Unfortunately, Peyton died in 1775 from an apoplectic stroke. He never lived to see his dream of overthrowing British rule fulfilled.

Before his death, Peyton resided in the family home, which overlooked Market Square where the military staged its demonstrations. The house was a center for the political and social activities of the gentry class. With its numerous outbuildings, it resembled a small plantation estate. Twenty-four slaves were required to run the household and attend to the many functions hosted by the family.

Construction on the oldest section of this white-frame house was begun in 1715 or 1716. Eventually, a section was added linking the house to another one John Randolph owned on the next lot. When John died in 1737, he deeded the house to his wife Susannah and after her death to their son Peyton.

The interior of the house showcases a great stairwell, a rare round-headed window, and many grand mirrors. On the second floor, there is an oak-paneled bedroom, which was quite unusual for colonial times.

Over the years, numerous stories have been told about dark, menacing spirits that dwell within the walls of this beautiful house. There is one particular story that may explain why so many fables of death and sorrow are connected to the Peyton Randolph House.

In 1745, Peyton married Elizabeth Harrison, who was also descended from one of Virginia's finest families. Betty, as she was known, was born to Colonel Benjamin Harrison and Anne Carter Harrison. Betty's grandfather was the wealthy Robert "King" Carter, who is discussed later in this book. Betty was raised on the James River on the lavish Berkeley Plantation with her six brothers and three sisters.

Because of her privileged upbringing, Betty was accustomed to getting her own way and had little tolerance for the misfortunes of others. She was also a strong-willed and determined woman.

One example of her determination came when she contracted a severe case of smallpox in 1781. A woman with a lesser will to live would have probably succumbed to the disease.

Betty was a well-educated woman, which was unusual for an eighteenth-century woman. She ran the Randolph household with an iron hand, and it was often the Randolph slaves that felt the brunt of her willfulness.

One of these slaves who probably suffered more than the others was Betty's own personal slave, Eve. Betty's daily fits of temper made Eve's life continuously miserable.

In 1775, Virginia's royal governor, Lord Dunmore, issued a proclamation that granted freedom to all slaves who ran away from their Patriot owners to join the British army. Even though it meant leaving a son behind, Eve joined eight other slaves in running away from the Randolph household.

Although no one is certain whether Eve was captured or returned voluntarily to be with her son, she was back with Betty Randolph five years later. Eve received a severe whipping, and her situation deteriorated to the point that she fled once again. This time she was seized within a year. We can only imagine what disciplinary action Eve faced on her second return.

When Betty died in late 1782, she left a special punishment for Eve in a codicil of her will. It stated "Whereas Eve's bad behaviour [has] laid me under the necessity of selling her. I order and direct the money she sold for may be laid out in purchasing two Negroes . . . in lieu of Eve."

The order to sell Eve was one of the most devastating things Betty could have done to her slave. Selling Eve would not only mean that she would be torn from her family, but that she might be sold into circumstances that were far more harsh than those she left.

When her new owner arrived, Eve put up quite a fight. She screamed and cried as the new owner ripped her from the arms of her son. Because she offered such fierce resistance, the new owner restrained Eve in a cruel and painful manner. Eve was laid, face down, over a horse's back. Then her wrists were tied to her ankles under the horse's belly. It was at this point that Eve made a threat no one would soon forget.

In a venomous tone, Eve vowed vengeance on all who inhabited her former home. Although we don't know what happened to Eve during the rest of her life, we do know that tragedy followed generations of residents of the Peyton Randolph House. Several people died suddenly or committed suicide within the house's linen-covered walls. Many believe that Eve's curse was responsible for these deaths.

During the 1960s and 1970s, the building was used as a lodging house. Guests were delighted to stay in an authentic eighteenth-century home. However, few people spent the entire night. One such man was Howard Kidman. Mr. Kidman was so fearful that he abandoned the home during his visit in the fall of 1968. He reported, "I was resting comfortably when awakened by the peculiar feeling that someone was tugging on my arm. Naturally, I assumed I was dreaming, so I rolled over and went back to sleep. A short while later, I awoke with a start! I was being shaken violently! As my eyes adjusted to the darkness, I could see that I was completely alone. I darted out of bed and ran as fast as I could. I didn't even go back to collect the things I'd left behind."

Probably one of the best and most credible witnesses to discuss the spirit of the Peyton Randolph House was one of the Revolutionary War's greatest heroes, the Marquis de Lafayette. He stayed in the home during his return visit to Williamsburg in 1824. He wrote of his ghostly encounter in a letter to a friend. He stated, "I considered myself fortunate to lodge in the home of a great man, Peyton Randolph. I remembered it to be a fine and elegantly decorated building in which I looked forward to residing while in Williamsburg. Upon my arrival, as I entered through the foyer, I felt a hand on my shoulder. It nudged me as if intending to keep me from entering. I quickly turned, but found no one there. The nights were not restful as the sounds of voices kept me awake for most of my stay."

Perhaps Eve's spirit had returned to carry out her menacing promise. Throughout the years, several ghostly figures have been seen roaming the empty halls. The old colonial home appears to be filled with dark spirits from all walks of life and many different time periods. Although we will probably never know just how many angry souls continue to call the Peyton Randolph House their home, we can assume that Eve may still be around to carry out her curse.

The Peyton Randolph House is located in the historic section of Williamsburg on the corner of Nicholson and North England Streets. Guided tours are given daily from 9:30 a.m. until 5:30 p.m. A pass is needed to tour the building. Call (757) 220-7645 for additional information.

Flickering Lights in the Governor's Palace

The Governor's Palace

FROM ITS COMPLETION in 1722 until 1775, the Governor's Palace was home to seven royal governors. Lord Dunmore, whose fear of a Patriot attack caused him to flee the palace early one morning, was the last royal governor to reside here. However, Lord Dunmore was not the last governor to call this palace home. Two governors of the newly formed Commonwealth of Virginia—Patrick Henry and Thomas Jefferson—also made the palace their official residence.

In 1780, the capital was moved to Richmond, leaving behind an abandoned palace. Nevertheless, the palace was not empty for long.

In late 1781, the siege of Yorktown created a need for hospital facilities. The abandoned palace was converted into a hospital for the critically injured victims who fought on the Patriot side of this brutal battle. On December 22, 1781, tragedy struck when the palace burned to the ground. One of the bedridden patients was killed. The historic building remained little more than a distant memory until the restoration of Williamsburg began in the late 1920s. At that point, plans were made to restore the grand building to its former place in the heart of the city.

When the original construction of the palace was first proposed, many thought it could never be done. Since much of Virginia was wilderness and most homes outside of Williamsburg were quite simple, constructing such an elaborate building was a great accomplishment.

By the late 1700s, the palace was magnificent indeed. As influential visitors entered the grand entrance hall, they were greeted by the royal coat of arms. Dozens of finely polished muskets hung in a circular pattern on the ceiling above their heads.

Leather and velvet furnishings, designed in the oriental style popular during the colonial period, decorated the many spacious rooms of the elegant three-story building. Hand-engraved swords and enormous portraits of royal family members hung on the walls. Large mirrors, reflecting candlelight, illuminated the building. A large mahogany desk stood in the library, which was stocked with hundreds of books. Valuable silver ornaments and gold-leafed china were placed throughout the palace. Imported-tile fireplaces warmed the building's open hallways.

Between 1749 and 1754, a supper room and the great ballroom were added. These new additions added a festive air to the palace. Dozens of fashionable guests would spend the evening dancing the minuet while the orchestra played the latest melodies.

The palace also included sixty-three acres of surrounding grounds. Balconies overlooked the elaborate gardens and allowed the sweet fragrance of Virginia boxwoods to waft through the building. The massive outer walls that surrounded the palace also enclosed a kitchen outbuilding, the stables, a coach house, and several other outbuildings.

By the early 1930s, the restoration of the palace and its gardens was underway. While rummaging through the gardens in an attempt to learn what vegetation had grown in Williamsburg's heyday, archaeologists made an astounding discovery. Among the roots and weeds, they discovered the remains of a human skeleton. As excited excavators continued to dig in an effort to learn more about the unidentified body, they discovered even more bodies. By the time they had finished, they had unearthed the remains of 156 men and two women from the palace gardens.

Mingled with the bodies were musket balls with deeply imbedded teeth marks. This discovery led the archaeologists to deduce that the bodies belonged to the patients who had been treated at the palace during its days as a hospital.

Because there was little anaesthesia during the Revolutionary War, the wounded suffered great agony. To distract the patient from pain, especially during an amputation, the wounded soldiers would bite down on lead balls. This did not stop the pain, but it did keep the suffering Patriots from biting off their tongues. This practice became the source for the term, "biting the bullet." The anguish these heroic men experienced during amputations is unimaginable to us today. Less than half of the soldiers who underwent an amputation would survive. Most died from blood loss, shock, or infection.

Although the musket balls helped the archaeologists to explain the existence of the male bodies, there were still some questions about the identities of the two female bodies.

Two theories emerged. Some people speculate that these women were family members of soldiers. During the Revolutionary War, women would often follow their husbands on their campaigns. They would set up camp, cook meals, tend the wounded, and do everything in their power to ease the burden of the fighting men.

A second theory is generally the more accepted explanation. This theory suggests that the women were nurses who died from one of the numerous diseases brought into the hospital by the soldiers. During the war, ten times more people lost their lives from disease than from combat.

Whoever these women may have been, there is evidence that their spirits have never left the palace. Although the palace is only used for exhibition purposes today, sometimes late at night an inexplicable flickering light can be seen passing from window to window on the third floor. Search as they might, no one has ever found the origin of this mysterious light.

Bruce Price, a security guard for Colonial Williamsburg, knows first hand that the palace contains an unknown spirit. During an interview, he stated, "One evening last year, as I was making my nightly rounds, I saw an odd light shining in the Governor's Palace. It seemed to be moving back and forth on the top floor. No one is allowed in the buildings after hours, so I decided to take a closer look to find out who was inside. As I made my way down the Palace Green, I could see the light looked to be a flame from a candle or lantern. It's a strict policy not to have any burning materials in the buildings because of the risk of fire.

"When I opened the palace door, everything was quiet. There was no sound at all. As I crept up the stairs, my heart felt like it was pounding out of my chest. I had visions of running into a vandal or thief. Luckily, I made it up the stairs without incident. However, I knew I still had to check all the rooms. As I made a room to room search, I grew more confident that no one was inside the palace. I have to admit, I was relieved.

"After I finished, I locked the palace door and began walking down the Palace Green. I felt a little silly for being so nervous about the whole thing. Just then, I turned to take one last look at the palace. A wave of adrenaline rushed through my body! The flickering light was passing from one room to the next, on the third floor!"

Although more than two centuries have passed, the ghosts of the devoted women appear to remain within the Governor's

Palace. As the spirits of the nurses continue to care for the wounded, who lie helpless in their sickbeds, it seems their dedication to duty transcends all barriers of time.

The Governor's Palace is situated in the historic section of Williamsburg at the end of the Palace Green. The green runs south to north, occupying two city blocks. It is clearly visible while strolling down Duke of Gloucester Street. Guided tours are given daily from 9:30 a.m. until 5:30 p.m. A pass is needed to tour the building, its outbuildings, and the grounds. Call (757) 220-7645 for information.

The Legend of Thomas Moore

The Henry Street Shops

IN THE EIGHTEENTH CENTURY, two very different brothers lived in the town of Williamsburg. The more stable of the
two, Horace Moore, lived in a comfortable little white house
on Henry Street. Quite content to live out his years in the
town of his birth, Horace vowed that he would never leave
Williamsburg.

Unfortunately, his sense of duty to the Southern cause during the Civil War caused him to rethink his plans. When he
left to join the Southern army, Horace wrote that he feared

he would never return. His predictions came true. Horace died in battle in the spring of 1864.

Horace left his residence on Henry Street to his only brother, Thomas. Thomas had completely different ideas about what to do with Horace's beloved home. Thomas was not content with small-town life. He was filled with wanderlust and a passion for beautiful ladies. This passion soon manifested itself in a "friendship" with a local woman named Constance Hall.

The only problem with this relationship was that Constance was married. Night after night, Constance would sneak away from her home and family to meet Thomas Moore at his little white house on Henry Street. The couple made no effort to conceal their meetings. It was only a matter of time before Constance's husband would find out about their trysts.

One Sunday morning, Harvey Hall finally paid an unexpected visit to the Moore residence. Having heard the rumors that were spreading all over town, Hall was not surprised to find his wife with Thomas Moore. A violent argument ensued over the young woman. When the argument was over, Thomas was dead.

Realizing that her husband had killed Moore and would probably be indicted for murder because of her misdeeds, Constance helped her husband hide Moore's body in the basement. Thomas's body was discovered eight days later, and Harvey Hall was accused of the slaying. Hall was convicted and imprisoned for life. Although Constance evaded prosecution, she was shunned by her former friends and neighbors. No one wanted anything to do with this shameless, adulterous woman.

She soon realized that she would have to leave town to make a fresh start. One night under cover of darkness, Constance fled Williamsburg. She was never heard from again. Her final whereabouts remain a mystery even today.

Constance's disappearance would end the sad saga except for the wandering spirit of Thomas Moore. As legend has it, Thomas still roams the darkened streets of Williamsburg in search of his love, Constance Hall. His dashing figure has been observed in local shops near the place where the Moore House used to stand.

One of Thomas's appearances occurred in a bookstore on Duke of Gloucester Street in the late 1980s. The manager of this store, Nancy Barker, was working on the day's receipts after all the other employees had gone home. Nancy said, "I was in my office in the back, when I heard a noise coming from the front area. I was sure I was the only person left inside, because I checked the store thoroughly before I locked up. I peeked around the corner and saw a man standing by one of the registers. I had no idea how he could have gotten in. He was dressed in black from head to toe, and his skin was a pale shade of white. In spite of his sickly color, I thought he was quite handsome.

"I ducked back into my office to call 911. I locked the door and sat crouched in the corner waiting for help. About five minutes later, I heard someone pounding on the front door. It was the police. I told them all the doors were locked, so the intruder still had to be inside. They searched the entire store, but couldn't find any trace of him."

Thomas made another appearance in October 1991. Mike Trumble, an employee of a local jewelry store on Henry Street, was also frightened by the spirit of the murdered man. "That evening, I stayed late to do inventory," Mike said. "I was sitting in the middle of the floor counting stock, when I heard a light tapping sound. As I stood up I saw a man with a dark mustache, peering in through the window. I noticed he was incredibly pale. He scanned the room as if he was looking for something in particular. As I watched him, he faded away before my eyes!"

It would seem the misguided spirit of Thomas Moore frantically searches for the woman who once made him happy in the little white house on Henry Street. Perhaps he never realized that the one true love in his life would eventually be the cause of his untimely death.

The Moore House was located where the Henry Street Shops now stand in Merchants Square. This quaint shopping center is near the corner of Henry and Francis Streets in Colonial Williamsburg. The shops carry a wide array of modern-day and colonial items. Many are open daily from 9:30 a.m. until 9:00 p.m.

Patriots Still Camp on the Tayloe House Grounds

The Tayloe House

WHILE WILLIAMSBURG was the capital of Virginia from 1699 to 1780, it attracted many of the wealthy and politically motivated citizens of the state. Students such as Thomas Jefferson attended the College of William and Mary. George Washington visited the Wythe House. Patrick Henry gave his passionate speeches inside the Capitol Building. It was a town filled with excitement until the simmering tensions with England came to a boil in the mid-1770s.

In the 1770s, thousands of colonists took up arms against the Mother Country. Patriot forces fought savage battles to win freedom for the colonies. Most of Williamsburg's population favored the struggle for independence. Those citizens who did not side with the Patriots were considered outcasts. Many were forced to flee to England for their safety.

During this time, Williamsburg became a place where fighting soldiers could get equipment repaired and horses shod. Townspeople supplied the Patriot soldiers with blankets, clothing, food, and lodging.

Military troops built a large encampment behind the Tayloe House on Nicholson Street. The land used for this encampment was owned by a local justice of the peace, Colonel John Tayloe. The two-story, white-framed house where John Tayloe lived was built between 1752 and 1759 for Dr. James Carter. In 1759, Colonel Tayloe purchased the property for three times the amount Carter paid.

The colonel's office was located on the grounds, east of the main house. It featured a bell-shaped roof that was quite uncommon for Williamsburg. The wooded lot behind the home was left to grow wild. Although Colonel Tayloe kept the lawn surrounding his house perfectly manicured, he allowed nature to take its course on the remainder of the property.

The Patriot forces found Colonel Tayloe's wooded property an excellent site for their encampment. Unfortunately, the colonel did not support the struggle for freedom. Even though he was a close personal friend of George Washington, he could not bring himself to support the Patriot cause. Unswayed by popular opinion, Tayloe was forced to resign from public office in 1776. In spite of his opinions, hundreds of weary soldiers continued to camp on the wooded lot behind his home.

During the attack against Lord Cornwallis at Yorktown, thousands of gallant revolutionaries spilled their blood in battle. Many of the wounded were brought back to the Tayloe House grounds for treatment. Some were fortunate enough to survive, but many others died here. Soon after this battle, the war effectively ended, leaving the bustling campsite deserted. Soon, there was no trace of the fighting men who once camped here.

Over 150 years later, the Tayloe grounds teamed with activity once again. For decades, Colonial Williamsburg used the property for military demonstrations. Cannon fire was heard daily. A constant stream of Revolutionary War reenactors marched across the historic lawn, just as the Patriots did two centuries ago.

After these exhibitions began, people reported hearing voices and laughter emanating from the former encampment during late night hours. The smell of campfires sometimes filled the air. Because spirits can stay dormant until they are awakened by a sudden flurry of activity, it is quite possible that these reenactments aroused the ghosts on the Tayloe House grounds.

In 1995, Pat Harris and his wife Gail came to Williamsburg for some much needed rest. "We thought strolling the streets of town in the cool winter months would be soothing," Pat remarked. "One night, we decided to brave the cold to learn more about Williamsburg's historic homes. As we walked through the streets with our map in hand, the sound of a crowd took us by surprise. People were laughing, singing, and having a good time. We wanted to join in on the fun, so we took off down the street in the direction of the festivities.

"When we reached what we now know as the Tayloe House, we saw the light from a bonfire. Our excitement grew as we scurried down the walk beside the home. Unfortunately, our enthusiasm fizzled when we reached the backyard. The grounds were empty, dark, and silent. Feeling let down, we returned to our hotel. Later, our excitement grew once again when we realized we had interrupted an event from the past."

It appears that the commotion generated by military presentations awakened the slumbering soldiers. It is indeed possible that the fallen men of Yorktown remain in their encampment, unaware they died in battle. On still nights, sounds of the revolution live on, giving us a glimpse into the past and reminding us of all the sacrifices that were made in the name of freedom.

The Tayloe House is located on the western end of Nicholson Street in Colonial Williamsburg.

The Loveless Lady of the Public Records Office

The Public Records Office

WHEN THE CAPITOL BUILDING burned in 1747, many of the colony's public records were destroyed. It took over a year to sort out the records that were not consumed by fire. After this catastrophe, colonial leaders decided it would be safer to house important documents in a separate building. This led to the construction in 1748 of the Public Records Office, which was also called the secretary's office. This historic structure is now the oldest archival building in North America.

To avoid a second blaze, the Public Records Office was made as fireproof as possible. On the design for the building, the architects specified that the builders not add an attic or basement. The interior walls were made of plaster laid on brick; the floor was made of stone. Using as little wood as possible in the construction, colonial architects hoped there would not be another fire. The building did have several fireplaces, however. They were used to warm the building and protect the documents from mold.

Although the Public Records Office was built to house important documents, it was also designed to impress high society with Virginia's prosperity. Glazed bricks blanket the outer walls, providing evidence of this prosperity. Before 1750, this costly decorative style was so expensive, it was only used by the most affluent builders. The rubbed brick surrounding the building's heavy double doors was used on the more elegant churches of that period. The original semicircular entrance steps were discovered in the 1930s when the office was being renovated. The two massive chimneys complete the effect of this imposing building.

Throughout the years, the Public Records Office has served many purposes. In 1784, it was converted into a grammar school. From 1789 to 1824, the building served as rental property. In 1824, it became an office for the clerk of Chancery Court. In 1855, it was acquired by the neighboring Female Academy, which was located on the grounds of the Capitol Building. In 1862, it played a role in the Civil War.

When 48,000 Southern troops made their escape from Yorktown, many Rebels took refuge inside the walls of this building. When the Union cavalrymen discovered the Rebel hiding place, they surrounded the building and fired on it until they were convinced the Confederates had run out of ammunition. The Union soldiers then burst through the doors of the building and captured the defenseless enemy. Numerous musketball holes blanket the Public Records Office, providing evidence of this skirmish.

Despite all of the precautions against fire, the building was burned during this turbulent time. An angry mob of runaway slaves broke through the wooden doors and set the building ablaze in an effort to destroy the records of their ownership. Because of its two-feet-thick walls, the sturdy structure remained standing.

Near the turn of the twentieth century, the structure became home to David Roland Jones and his family. Jones and his wife had seven children—all girls. Although a large family was typical in the early twentieth century, this family was unusual because none of the young ladies ever married or even left home. They lived within the confines of their home their entire lives.

The girls would dress in long-flowing gowns and meticulously fix their hair, just to spend the day on the lawn with their many cats. People have speculated that the lack of freedom that these young ladies experienced was due to their unusually strict father.

What is certain is that David Roland Jones came from a strict religious background, since several of his ancestors were clergymen with strong feelings about what was right and wrong. Perhaps Mr. Jones's stern beliefs led him to effectively hold his daughters prisoners in their own home.

The dictatorial father thought so highly of his home, he had his family buried less than twenty feet away. A high brick wall encloses the small graveyard. The wall keeps intruders out, but it seems there is one person it cannot keep in—one of Jones's own daughters. It is commonly believed that long after her death, the spirit of Edna Jones still remains confined to the grounds of her home.

Growing up in a strict household, Edna became increasingly restless as the years went by. When she was a young woman of eighteen, she grew more unhappy with every passing day. Desperately wanting a family of her own, Edna grew more and more depressed. She thought her dreams of marriage would never be fulfilled without an opportunity to find companionship. She needed to escape the restraints of her home, if only for a short while.

Since she was a shy, quiet girl, Edna was too timid to stand up to her father. She feared his reaction. Although Mr. Jones was not considered a physically abusive man, his threats of violence terrified Edna.

It was during this time that John Mince made weekly trips to the Jones home to deliver food and supplies to the reclusive family. Edna looked forward to John's visits with great anticipation. Deep in her heart, she knew she was falling in love with him. Unbeknownst to her, John felt the same way.

Then one summer day, John boldly proclaimed his feelings to Edna. For one brief moment her happiness knew no bounds. She then realized her father would never allow this budding romance to blossom. Anticipating Mr. Jones's opposition, the couple made plans to meet on the grounds of the Governor's Palace. Since the palace had burned over a century earlier, the grounds would be deserted.

Impatiently, Edna awaited darkness before dressing in her finest clothes and piling her reddish hair neatly on her head. She crept into the night to rendezvous with her newfound beau. The farther she walked, the more panic she felt. She was sure her father would kill her if he ever found out. Unfortunately, Edna's fear caused her to ignore the oncoming carriage that was approaching at a deadly speed. That night, the lovesick lady lost her life under the wheels of a speeding coach.

It is thought, however, that Edna's frightened spirit frantically rushed home. Unaware of her own death, her ghost was only concerned about the thrashing she would receive if her deception was discovered. Since that tragic night, witnesses have sighted her slender figure roaming the property of the old Public Records Office. Her illuminated silhouette has been known to make sudden appearances, only to vanish two or three seconds later.

At times, Edna's apparition hovers over the graves in the Jones family cemetery. She seems to fade in and out at will. Her glowing ghost has been photographed inside the graveyard where her body rests. Strangers have heard lonely Edna calling out as they make their way through the property.

An entry in Agnus Taylor's diary dated October 5, 1969, provides testimony of Edna's floating spirit. Agnus stated "Today, while working in the Public Records Office, I came upon a frightening discovery! As I was scrubbing the windows, I saw the vision of a woman in white, dangling in mid-air over the old graveyard. She was suspended about five feet off the ground. Then after a moment or two, she disappeared. Even though the vision was fleeting, I'm sure of what I saw!"

While giving a "Haunted Williamsburg Tour" of this property, I also experienced a strange event. I had just described the building when one spectator interrupted, claiming the ghost of a young woman was hiding behind a corner of the historic structure. This tourist, Linda Oswald, said, "The spirit is dressed in a long white or light-blue gown. Her red hair is woven tightly around her head. She seems to be frightened or shy, and has severe problems with her eyes. She ducks behind the building whenever she thinks I've seen her."

Later, Linda's husband told us that his wife was known for her ability as a psychic. He claimed that Linda has even worked with the Philadelphia Police Department on several occasions to help them retrieve clues for various crimes.

Soon after, I saw an old picture of Edna and realized that Linda Oswald's description of Edna Jones's eyes was correct. Until that time, I had no knowledge that Edna wore thick glasses. Early in the century, women wore eyeglasses only if they had extreme vision impairment. It was quite unusual to see women adorned with eyewear.

Another Williamsburg visitor, Karen Curry, also had an unusual story to tell abut her experience on the grounds of the Public Records Office. Karen related, "I was walking through the property early one morning, when I heard the name 'Dora, Dora,' excitedly being called out to me. I turned to see who was there, but after searching the entire property, I was convinced I was alone. Later, I was told the neighbor and close personal friend of the Jones family for several decades was Dora Armistead. After talking with someone who remembers Dora when she was young, it seems her physical characteristics and my own are strikingly similar. Who knows, this may have been a case of mistaken identity on the part of the lady who haunts the graveyard."

Perhaps the lonely Edna Jones doesn't realize that all the people in her life have long since passed away. If this is true, she will continue to walk the quiet grounds of the Public Records Office, frightening unsuspecting strangers for many years to come.

The Public Records Office stands at the eastern end of Duke of Gloucester Street in Colonial Williamsburg. It is located to the north of the Capitol Building. The building houses exhibits. A pass is required.

Dora Armistead Protests Her Move

The former home of Dora Armistead

THE ARMISTEADS were truly one of Virginia's first families. William Armistead came to the colony in 1635. By 1651, he owned 1,213 acres of land in Virginia. The family's great wealth was passed from generation to generation until the Civil War. At that time, most of the family's money and property was confiscated by the Union Army, leaving the family heir, Cary Peyton Armistead, homeless.

Cary persevered, however, and by 1889, he had accumulated enough funds to purchase a one-and-a-half-story home, located next to the Public Records Office in Williamsburg.

Unfortunately, he had been duped in the deal. He later found out the building was infested with termites and was about to collapse. In 1891, Cary had the dilapidated structure torn down to the foundations and replaced with a grand twelve-room Victorian home. The foundations were all that remained of an eighteenth-century coffee house and tavern that had once stood on the property.

Every room of Cary's new three-story home had a large fireplace. Several rooms had French marble mantles. The ceilings were extremely high to keep the house cool in summer. The front portion of the building had a long covered porch, which wrapped around to the side entrance where Cary kept his law office.

In the years that followed, Cary and his wife Endora had five children. Sadly, Mr. Armistead died in 1901, leaving his family destitute. Endora was forced to take a job at the Public Hospital to support her family. Her eldest soon died at the age of twenty, but Endora managed to raise enough money to put all four surviving children through college. The two male children became lawyers; the two females, teachers. For much of their adult lives, all four offspring resided at the Armistead home.

During the acquisition and restoration of the town, Endora refused to sell to Colonial Williamsburg, no matter how much money they offered her. She stood strong and was eventually the only one in the neighborhood to keep her property. Endora was convinced her house would be torn down to rebuild the eighteenth-century buildings that once stood on the grounds. Her obstinacy most surely saved the family home from demolition.

After the deaths of Endora and her two surviving sons, sisters Dora and Cara continued to dwell in the family residence. To make ends meet, the sisters later turned the home into an inn. For decades, the sisters operated the lodging house until they grew too old to manage it.

Dora, or "Miss Dora" as she was commonly called, was perfectly happy living the quiet, peaceful life Williamsburg offered prior to the restoration period. Unfortunately for her, as the city's renovations continued into the 1950s and 1960s, more and more tourists flooded the town. Whereas Cara saw the tourists as paying customers, Dora became increasingly agitated by the flurry of activity.

In 1979, Cara died, leaving Dora completely alone. Dora lived until 1984, when she died at the age of ninety-three. After Dora's death, the Association for the Preservation for Virginia turned the house into a historic house museum, but in recent years it has been unoccupied. While the house stood unoccupied, it seemed to hold a mysterious secret within its walls. From one day to the next, at some time during the night, something would shift the curtains in Dora's second-floor bedroom window from one side to the other. This proved to many that Dora's feisty spirit continued to dwell inside her former home.

Then, in November 1995, Colonial Williamsburg leased the property and had the huge yellow house moved from its location on Duke of Gloucester Street to North Henry Street.

From events that followed, it would seem Dora's ghost was unhappy with her new address. While passing the home, a local woman, Elaine Barrette, noticed a crowd had gathered. They were staring excitedly at the empty building.

"When I joined them," Elaine explained, "I could see the curtains in the upstairs window were blowing furiously even though all the windows and doors appeared to be tightly shut. Since there weren't any electrical wires leading to the house, it seemed impossible for it to have been a fan or heater. None of us could explain what we were seeing.

"Since that time, I've made it a practice to pass the home every few days. One day the curtains in the second-floor window are pulled to the left; the next, they're pulled to the right. The building is still unoccupied and has no electrical wires running to its rooms."

In another instance, Tracy Chamberlain, a friend of mine, came to town one winter for Grand Illumination. She had a story to tell about an ominous house she and her husband James passed while walking North Henry Street. She said, "I'll tell you, there are a few homes in Williamsburg I would be afraid to live in. My husband and I passed an eery house that looked like it had been moved. It stood up off the ground. When we walked in front of it, I made my husband switch places with me because I felt someone was staring at me from one of the darkened second-floor windows. I had the worst feeling, and the hair on my neck stood on end. There is no way anyone could ever make me go into that building!" Later, I discovered that Tracy was referring to Dora Armistead's house.

It would seem that Dora is still angered by visitors passing along the street in front of her home. She sends out silent vibrations to discourage visiting tourists. Apparently, Miss Armistead has not let death keep her from expressing her displeasure.

The Dora Armistead House is located near the corner of North Henry and Scotland Streets, one block north of Merchants Square. The building is not owned by Colonial Williamsburg and is not open to the public. You can, however, see it clearly from the road. The house remains unoccupied and padlocked to this very day.

Long-Ago Lovers Unite in the George Wythe House

The George Wythe House

EVEN BY TODAY'S STANDARDS, the George Wythe House remains one of Colonial Williamsburg's most opulent houses. Built in the mid-eighteenth century, this spacious, two-story, brick building had a prestigious location overlooking the Palace Green.

The restored house has four rooms on each floor. Each floor is divided by a grand stairwell. All of the rooms have a separate fireplace, and each of the bedrooms has a painted, four-poster bed adorned with a flowing canopy.

The interior has extensive masonry work that gives each room its own unique charm. Brightly colored wallpaper, accentuated by bold trim, lines the halls. At one time, it was thought that color schemes used in colonial homes were subdued. This theory was proven wrong when a sample of the original wallpaper was found in the Wythe House. It was anything but subtle.

Like the Peyton Randolph House, the Wythe House resembled a small plantation estate. Among the buildings on the property were a laundry, a lumber house, a poultry house, a well, stable, and a kitchen. A beautifully manicured lawn, a kitchen garden, and an orchard added elegance to the grounds. The Wythe House became one of the most duplicated homes in America.

George Wythe acquired use of the property as a wedding gift from his father-in-law, Richard Taliaferro. Wythe was a man of many accomplishments. He was a lawyer, a judge, a teacher, speaker of the House of Delegates, and a signer of the Declaration of Independence. He was also a great supporter of the Patriot cause. In 1806, Wythe died a painful, lingering death when his grandnephew, George Wythe Sweeney, supposedly poisoned Wythe so he could gain his inheritance.

Just prior to the siege of Yorktown, George Washington used the Wythe House as his temporary headquarters. After the siege, the house accommodated dozens of wounded men who fell during the battle. A young French soldier named Colonel Oscar LaBlanc was one of these men. He was making a swift recovery when he suddenly took a turn for the worse. A local woman named Katherine Anderson watched over the sick officer night and day. She was completely dedicated to the dying man, spending every waking moment by his side. When Colonel LaBlanc was no longer in danger of dying, the couple made plans to marry.

Anticipating her wedding, Katherine was blissfully happy. Her love for the French hero grew stronger every passing day. Unfortunately, Oscar contracted malaria from one of the other patients in the temporary hospital. As Oscar grew sicker, Katherine nursed him constantly. This time, she could not save him. Oscar died one week after contracting malaria.

Katherine's grief was unbearable; she seemed to lose the will to carry on. It wasn't long before the bereaved young woman passed away from "natural causes." Rumors said she died of a broken heart.

For decades, workers and tourists alike have become frighteningly aware of a ghostly presence that lurks in the George Wythe House. Many have heard voices and footsteps coming from the second floor. At night, shadowy figures walk the house's darkened hallways.

Richard Lucus, an interpreter for Colonial Williamsburg, told of his haunting experience in this old colonial home. "About three years ago, while I was working alone on the second floor, I heard someone call out my name. The voice was unfamiliar, but I was drawn towards it, nevertheless. As I rounded the corner, I saw the dark outline of a man standing in the hallway. I asked him what he wanted, but he didn't answer. Then, right in front of my eyes, he dissolved into thin air! Since then, I insist that I not work alone in the Wythe House."

Kitty Martin, a visitor to the home about the same time that Mr. Lucus had his ghostly encounter, had one of her own. Kitty said, "I was looking into one of the bedrooms on the second floor, when I saw a woman dressed in colonial clothing, standing quietly in the corner. She seemed upset. I turned to call to my sister, but when I looked back, the woman was gone. There was no door leading out of the room except for the one I was standing by, and I know she didn't pass me. All that remained was the strong smell of antiseptic."

Evidence suggests the brokenhearted spirit of Katherine Anderson has returned to the house where she lost her true love. However, there may be a happy ending to this otherwise sad story. It may well be that the souls of the long-ago lovers have reunited within the George Wythe House, sharing the love in death that fate stole from them in life.

The George Wythe House is located on the corner of Palace and Prince George Streets in Colonial Williamsburg. It stands on the western side of the Palace Green. The building is usually open to the public. However, many of Colonial Williamsburg's buildings are closed one or more days a week, so it is advisable to call (757) 220-7645 to learn if it will be open on the day of your visit. A pass is required to tour the home and its grounds.

Colonial Festivities Continue at the Raleigh Tavern

The Raleigh Tavern

THE RALEIGH TAVERN was one of the most popular taverns in eighteenth-century Virginia. Built around 1717, the tavern's reputation as a social gathering place grew with every passing year.

The tavern began as a small pub. Originally, it was only half of its present size. As the Raleigh's popularity increased, additions were constructed to accommodate the overflow of patrons. Businessmen, politicians, and townspeople came to the tavern to learn about current events and catch up on local gossip. Slaves and other goods were sold on its steps; lectures and auctions were held inside.

Colonial Virginians were known to gamble a great deal. From

the evidence of dice boxes discovered during excavations of the property, it appears gambling was a frequent activity at the tavern. Fortunes were known to change hands over a game of billiards, or even a mere game of checkers. The morning after John Custis, a local butcher, suffered heavy gambling losses, he was found with his throat cut. The coroner ruled the death a suicide.

Many important decisions about the Patriots' revolt against unfair British rule also took place at the Raleigh. When the governor dissolved the House of Burgesses in 1769 and again in 1774 for their disrespectful talk, Thomas Jefferson, Patrick Henry, George Washington, and others resumed their discussions in this building. Some of the plans for the Revolutionary War, including strategies for the siege of Yorktown, were formulated within the Raleigh's walls.

The Raleigh was not just a place for politics and gambling; it also hosted many gala events. During public times, the time when court was in session, the tavern held grand balls for the socially elite. In the famous Apollo Room, dozens of George Washington's closest friends gave him a surprise birthday party. In 1776, Patrick Henry was honored by Virginia troops for his tireless efforts on behalf of the revolutionary cause with a parade followed by a night at the Raleigh. Almost every evening, the sounds of drinking and festivity emanated from this colonial hot spot.

After more than a century of merriment, the Raleigh Tavern celebrated one of its last grand events. In 1824, the Marquis de Lafayette visited Williamsburg. An enormous banquet was held at the tavern in his honor. Although he was sixty-seven years old, it seems Lafayette still enjoyed a rollicking evening. From that time on, however, the number of festivities dwindled at the Raleigh. Gala gatherings were virtually nonexistent.

In December 1859, the historic structure burned to the ground, taking with it memories of Williamsburg's flamboyant past. Between 1929 and 1932, the tavern was rebuilt on the original foundations to resemble its appearance during its former glory days. The impressive, elongated wooden tavern is painted white. Above the door frame hangs a lead bust of its namesake, Sir Walter Raleigh. Seven dormer windows line the front portion of the second floor. The lower portion has three windows on each side of the doorway. Dark shutters surround the first-floor windows, adding an air of classic elegance.

Three years before the fatal fire, a man named Samuel Armistead wrote in a letter to a friend about a haunting experience he had at the Raleigh Tavern. He was walking his dog one cold January evening when he was "attracted to the building by the sounds of voices, laughter, and strange music." He stated, "This was odd because the Raleigh has remained quiet for many years. The old tavern was dark and yet I heard the sounds of a party. As I got closer, I could smell pipe tobacco. I was overwhelmed by curiosity, so I approached the window to peek inside. From the dim light of a street lamp, I could see the building was completely empty! I must admit, I feared for my sanity."

One might assume the ghostly happenings attached to the

Raleigh Tavern would perish with the original building, but apparently they did not. With the tavern's reconstruction came the spirits of its past. As I was conducting interviews for the "Haunted Williamsburg Tour," I came upon a story almost identical to that of Samuel Armistead.

Dan Arnold, a custodian for Colonial Williamsburg, was embarrassed to tell of his experience with the tavern, thinking no one would believe him. Finally, Dan reluctantly told his story. He said, "I was working in the back of the Raleigh late one evening, when I heard noises coming from inside. I thought someone had broken in, so I decided to check it out. As I crept closer, I heard laughter and music. The music wasn't like anything we hear today; it was music of the eighteenth century—you know, spinets and harpsichords. Then I heard the clinking of glasses and the shuffling of feet. The strangest thing of all was the smell of pipe tobacco seeping from the cracks of the window casings. When I looked inside, everything stopped! The tavern was completely empty except for some painting equipment left by Colonial Williamsburg."

As I told him about Samuel Armistead's episode in 1856, a look of relief swept over Dan's face. He was relieved to hear he was not the only person who experienced this phenomenon. Now when he hears the sounds of a party emanating from the empty, darkened tavern, he no longer doubts his sanity.

The Raleigh Tavern is located on the east end of Duke of Gloucester Street. It is one of many hostelries situated just west of the Capitol

Building. Unlike the other taverns, the Raleigh does not serve dinner. However, it does have an excellent bakery on the property. The Raleigh is open to the public daily for guided tours from 9:30 a.m. until 5:30 p.m. A pass is required. Call (757) 220-7645 for details.

The Ghost Cat

Samantha, the ghost cat

GHOSTS HAUNT the earth for several reasons. If great sorrow is associated with the death, the victims may remain tied
to the location from the shock of their death. These spirits
may even be unaware of their own untimely demise. Some
apparitions may simply be too frightened to enter unknown
realms.

Many ghosts are afraid to move on because they fear punishment for misdeeds they performed in life awaits them on
the other side. Spirits may also linger because they believe
their work on this planet is not completed. Great love causes

wandering souls because the lovers can't bear to leave their grieving loved ones behind. Some people believe there is a black hole in time, allowing the past to exist with the present in a parallel dimension. This explains why events from yesteryear occur in the present.

Some locations attract ghosts like a magnet attracts iron. Williamsburg is believed to be one of those places. Perhaps this is due to the great upheaval that took place here, or perhaps the area has a supernatural pull coming from its ancient grounds. Whatever the reason, this historic landscape is known far and wide for its apparitions.

It seems that many of Williamsburg's spirits are not of the human species. Animal ghosts haunt the colonial capital as well. Gena Grant, a resident of Williamsburg, tells the story of her beloved cat, Samantha. Although Gena and her husband Stan have had several pets, Samantha was their favorite.

Samantha was a fun-loving animal who frolicked in the fields near the Grant home. The couple spent nine wonderful years with their beloved cat before tragedy struck. They discovered that Samantha had a tumor embedded in her neck. Although she was not in pain, the veterinarian told the couple that Samantha would need constant attention. Gena loved her cat so much, she was willing to do anything to make her cat's last year a comfortable one.

"Stan had built a little bed on top of Sam's favorite scratching post, but since her illness, she could no longer jump," Gena explained. "It was a foot and a half off the ground, so Samantha woke me several times a night to lift her back into bed. Samantha repeatedly nudged me from my sleep with her cold wet nose."

Sadly, one day Stan realized Samantha was too ill to carry on. The couple reluctantly brought their beloved pet to the veterinary hospital to put her out of her misery. Both Gena and Stan were heartsick over the loss of their furry family member.

"Later that night, after we had gone to bed, I felt a cold wet nose nudging against my cheek," Gena continued. "Since I was waking from a deep sleep, I momentarily forgot that Samantha had died. I saw Sam's darkened figure standing at the foot of our bed, but as I moved towards her, she just faded away."

Although it has been several years since Sam's demise, the Grant family still grieves over their loss. Gena says, "We do find comfort in the fact that Samantha's spirit remains with us. We see her regularly, frolicking in the fields near our home."

Since the first time Gena saw Sam's spirit, the ghost cat has continued her nightly visits to the couple's bed. She affectionately nudges Gena awake, only to vanish before Gena's eyes. To the Grants, this proves that separation by death has not ended their cat's everlasting love.

Williamsburg is known for its animal hauntings. Few cities can boast of so many documented cases of beloved family pets that have returned to earth after their death. Since the Grant home is located in the Williamsburg city limits, Gena can be certain her animal ghost is not the only one roaming the open fields of town.

The Death of
Martha Washington

Former home of the Custis family

MARTHA DANDRIDGE was born on June 2, 1731. Her father, a wealthy tobacco planter, built a magnificent estate on the Pamunkey River in central Virginia. He named it Chestnut Grove. Her mother, Frances, believed that education beyond the basics was not necessary for young women. However, she did believe an education in the social graces would prove advantageous. It appears Frances was correct, for Martha met her first husband, Daniel Parke Custis, at a gala affair held at the Governor's Palace. She was only sixteen at the time.

Daniel swept Martha off her feet with his charming ways. Having lived an isolated life, which left her unaccustomed to flattery, Martha was infatuated with the aggressive stranger who was twenty years her senior. In spite of the protests from Daniel's father, the couple married two years later in June 1749.

Since the couple's net worth was six million dollars, they lived quite comfortably wherever they chose. They owned several dwellings, including a green house across from Bruton Parish Church in Williamsburg. In 1714, Daniel's father, John Custis, purchased the land on which the house was built. After his father's death, Daniel inherited the house, which overlooked the Palace Green.

Several years passed in which the Custis family was blissfully happy. The Custises, who eventually had four children, led lives filled with grand balls and parties. They also enjoyed a high degree of social respectability. Then, out of nowhere tragedy struck. In the winter of 1751, the couple's oldest child, Daniel, died suddenly from illness. He was laid to rest in the Bruton Parish Church graveyard.

The Bruton Parish Church was the church of choice for many of the members of Williamsburg's high society. The original Bruton Parish Church was completed in 1683. When Williamsburg became the capital, a much larger church was needed. The grand building standing on the site today was built in 1715.

During the church's renovation in 1903–7, workers found an eighteenth-century burial ground for the socially and politically elite of the colonial period beneath the floor. Several bodies lay below the feet of parishioners for well over a century without being discovered.

Most of the identities of those buried in the cemetery outside the church are lost beneath the ground forever. The names of the dead which were etched on the stone or wooden markers used in early colonial days have long since disappeared. Later, elaborate grave markers, many imported from England, immortalized the dead. It is one of these imported markers that adorns the grave of young Daniel Custis.

After their son's death, the Custis family dropped out of the social rounds and lived a reclusive lifestyle. Although joy was gradually restored to their lives, their happiness was short-lived. In the spring of 1757, another tragedy befell this unfortunate family. Their little girl, Frances, died at the tender age of four, leaving her father devastated. She was buried in the same grave as her brother, which was a common practice in colonial times.

Frances was the light of her father's eye, and he had once said he would die if anything ever happened to her. True to his word, he took to his sickbed and refused to leave it for six months. By October, he died from a broken heart. Martha wrote, "At the moment of Daniel's death, the wind stopped, the birds quieted, and everything became deadly still. Not a sound could be heard. Even the clock stopped, as if frozen in time." Although Martha never understood these strange happenings, they left such a strong impression that she continued to relate this story to others for the rest of her life.

At the young age of twenty-six, Martha Custis was left with a fortune, hundreds of slaves, numerous land holdings, and two fatherless children. She then met Colonel

George Washington at a dinner party. After almost a year of courtship, they married on January 6, 1759.

It seemed that Martha was fated to endure great sorrow. A few years later, she lost a third child to illness, despite the care of several costly physicians. Patsy Custis died during an epileptic seizure in 1773.

Despite this latest tragedy, George and Martha lived happily until duty called. George was selected to lead the Patriots in their fight against tyrannical British rule. As a good wife of the revolution, Martha served her husband by doing whatever she could to ease his burden. She often worked in the army encampments, even though exposure to the elements took a toll on her health.

Martha's last surviving child, John Custis, who was nicknamed Jacky, followed his heroic stepfather into battle. He died at Yorktown from camp fever. While George should have been celebrating his victory at Yorktown in 1781, he was mourning the loss of his beloved stepson.

After the war ended, the Washingtons wanted nothing more to do with public life. Their only wish was to retire to Mount Vernon to live a simple existence. Unfortunately, this was not meant to be. George was called to be the president of the new country. Selflessly, George and Martha sacrificed several more years of personal happiness for their country.

They were married for four decades until George's death in 1799. After George's death, it was Martha who took to her bed, refusing to leave it for two long years. Each day, she piled George's love letters over her like a quilt, reading them time and time again. Then one day, servants found Martha tearing the letters up at a feverish pitch. It was as if she knew something was about to happen.

Martha had shredded all but one letter when a shocked look swept over her face. With her eyes fixed on the ceiling she lay motionless, clutching the last remaining letter to her chest. She sat up and spoke the name, "George," as if she were looking into the face of her late husband. Then, the curves of her mouth turned upwards into a peaceful smile, as she lay back for eternal sleep.

Martha Washington's first two children lay buried in the Bruton Parish Church graveyard in Colonial Williamsburg. This large church is located on the corner of Duke of Gloucester and Palace Streets, adjacent to the Palace Green. The church and graveyard are open to the public. There is no charge. The Custis family graves are situated next to the back wall of the church.

The former home of the Custis family is directly across the street from Bruton Parish Church on Duke of Gloucester Street. The home is not open to the public but can be viewed from the street.

The Battle of Williamsburg Rages On

Monument to Battle of Williamsburg

LIFE IN THE ENCHANTING WORLD of present-day Colonial Williamsburg is a wonderful blend of history, beautiful landscapes, and modern culture. Touring the historic streets of the city, a person can learn a great deal about the eighteenth century. Although you might not hear too much about Williamsburg during the nineteenth century, there was one horrific battle that took place here during the Civil War.

On May 5, 1862, a savage hand-to-hand battle was fought on the city's small streets and in the countryside a few miles outside of Williamsburg. Of the 40,000 soldiers engaged in the fight, almost 4,000 men were killed; thousands more were wounded.

The Battle of Williamsburg began early on a cold, wet morning. The woods were so thick that it was impossible to see if friend or foe was approaching. Both sides fought fiercely during a steady downpour of rain. Both armies were soon lost in the confusion. The torrential downpour caused poor visibility, and mud covered the identifying colors of the soldiers' uniforms. These factors caused mistakes in identification that often proved deadly. The thick underbrush was littered with the dead and wounded from both sides. Bodies lay upon bodies.

As the battle raged on, many soldiers resorted to using their bayonets because of a lack of ammunition. Confusion, fatigue, discouragement, and hand-to-hand combat all served to increase the fury of the fighting. Some soldiers wandered aimlessly on the battlefield, while others simply threw down their guns and ran away. Many hid in shrubs and bushes, hoping they would not be discovered until the fighting ended. With little or no direction from their leaders, the armies fumbled through the dense forest for over ten long hours of combat.

The battle also produced great acts of heroism and bravery. The valiant 24th Virginia screamed the rebel yell as its soldiers turned to meet the Union forces head on. The company lost most of its officers and almost half of its men during this stand. They charged a much larger enemy force with great courage, allowing their comrades to escape to safety.

One young Federal soldier, weakened by the loss of blood

from several wounds, guided three captured Confederate officers to a local prison. Despite his weakened state, the young hero held the officers' swords under the remnants of his mangled arm the entire way.

When the battle began, the people of Williamsburg ran to the battlefield to watch the fight. Many of the spectators stood under umbrellas as they watched the battle. Newspapermen went among the fighting soldiers to sell their wares. What many townspeople thought would be an interesting spectacle became horrifying as they watched hundreds of men dying while others lay on the muddy ground screaming in agony.

During the bloodiest part of the battle, the Rebels began their retreat. At this point the retreating forces became entangled with the onlookers. The panicked citizens were soon covered in mud and blood as they scrambled for safety.

By the end of the day, Union forces controlled the field. That night, General Joseph Johnston led the Confederates out of town under the cover of darkness. The Rebels left the town of Williamsburg in the hands of the Federals. They left their dead and wounded soldiers on the battlefield.

Later that night, the people of Williamsburg groped around in the murky darkness of the dense woods as they searched for wounded soldiers. The battlefield was a dreadful sight. In some places there were up to sixty bodies piled one on top of another. Some bodies were completely immersed in mud; others were hidden under branches and logs. Injured soldiers were still being found on the third day after the battle.

On the third night after the battle, a fire spread rapidly

through the woods. The torturous cries, which emanated from the flame-ridden field, wiped away any hope of finding more live victims.

Since those bleak days, the land where the conflict took place has been cleared; houses have been built. Some people who live in those homes today believe the furious fight still rages, as if trapped in time. The homeowners speak of spine-tingling events that still occur on the grounds of this tragic battlefield.

One couple, Betty and Sam Littleton, has lived on the battle-field for two decades. At first, they knew nothing of the events that happened on their property over one hundred years earlier. Now, they experience inexplicable occurrences on an almost daily basis.

"When we first moved in, we were awakened by the sound of people running through our yard," says Betty Littleton. "I was scared half to death by a bloodstained face staring at me through the bedroom window. From time to time, when we're sitting in the living room, the sounds of gunfire and cannons jolt us from our chairs. Sometimes, we hear bloodcurdling screams in the middle of the night. The sounds of clashing sabers and the moans of wounded soldiers keep us awake. At times, we sit on our back porch just to watch the ghostly happenings unfold before our eyes.

"These things don't bother me anymore, but they sure did at first. It took a long time for me to feel comfortable living in this house, but now I wouldn't live anywhere else. Where else can you get this kind of entertainment in your own backyard?"

While Betty Littleton views these hauntings with humor, her husband Sam pities the wandering souls of the Battle of Williamsburg. He says, "The most disturbing thing of all is the spirit of a young Confederate soldier running from tree to tree, as if he's hiding from the enemy. It's hard to imagine that this poor man has been suspended in a constant state of terror for well over a century.

"One night we awoke to the sound of excited voices. Then, all of a sudden, we heard a rope snap, like someone was being hanged. It was awful! I truly believe the Battle of Williamsburg continues to be fought in our backyard every single day."

As the years pass, little has changed on the Littletons' property. Time has done nothing to quiet the site of this horrendous battle. If anything, the reoccurrences have increased. It would seem the slaughtered soldiers of the Battle of Williamsburg remain suspended in time, doomed to walk the scene of their brutal deaths.

The most savage fighting during the Battle of Williamsburg took place about a mile east of the historic section of town. The only reminders of this battle are an obscure plaque off Pocahontas Trail on the grounds of Quarterpath Park and a small monument standing by the last visible redoubt on Penniman Road.

Pocahontas Trail and Penniman Road are both located approximately one-half mile east of the historic area. To reach the monument, you follow Penniman Road for a little over a mile.

Suicide at the
Public Hospital

The Public Hospital

WHEN THE PUBLIC HOSPITAL for Persons of Insane and Disordered Minds on Francis Street opened its doors in 1773, it was the first public institution in colonial America devoted exclusively to the care of the mentally ill. The original large brick building contained twenty-four cells, an apartment/office, and a meeting room for the supervising court of directors. In the beginning, the structure averaged between six and fifteen troubled patients.

From its opening until the later part of the nineteenth century, the compound grew to accommodate an increasing number of patients. It grew to include eight additional buildings on four acres of grounds.

For the first seven decades of the hospital's existence, patients inhabiting the asylum were clothed, fed, and treated using the accepted practices of the day. Although some patients were cured, some of the methods that were used during this time seem harsh and cruel by present standards.

The patients endured long periods of confinement and isolation. Their small, barred cells only had one tiny window for light. The patients slept on the floor on dirty straw-filled mattresses. Many were shackled to the walls. Woeful cries emanated from every room. The living quarters for the mentally ill were cold, damp, and drafty. Little warm clothing and few blankets were provided to keep them warm.

Inmates were forced to take large amounts of drugs. Some were dunked in cold water with their hands and feet tied. Others were jolted with electricity. Some were bled.

In 1841, one man changed the conditions in the asylum dramatically. Twenty-one-year-old Dr. John Minson Galt II became the last of four generations of Galts to be the asylum's superintendent. By that time, there was a general change in mental health care that focused on "moral management." For over twenty years, Galt worked tirelessly to improve the lives of his patients. Since he had no wife or children of his own, he truly thought of the inmates as family.

Dr. Galt believed the mentally ill should be treated with kindness and understanding. There were no more shackles on the walls. Patients became involved in social activities and even learned to play musical instruments. There were no more dirty mattresses on the floor. Patients were given clean beds, plenty of blankets to keep them warm, and three square meals a day. More buildings were erected to alleviate overcrowding. The inmates seemed to come alive under the care of this kind doctor.

After the Battle of Williamsburg in the spring of 1862, Federal troops took control of the town for three long years. When they invaded the city, the Union soldiers took over the hospital as well. Dr. Galt was physically removed from office, expelled from the asylum, and warned never to return. This devastated the dedicated humanitarian.

As he watched the living conditions of his beloved patients deteriorate, Dr. Galt suffered greatly. Some patients who were locked in their rooms died from neglect. Others were set free to wander the countryside with no place to go. Unsure of what course of action he could take to help these souls, the good doctor was filled with hopelessness. Two weeks after his dismissal, he was found dead in his home on the grounds of the hospital. He had taken an overdose of laudanum. The compassionate healer had ingested such a massive amount of the medication that many vessels in his brain had burst, leaving a large pool of blood on the wooden floor.

Soon after, the Lee family moved into Dr. Galt's former home. Mrs. Lee wrote, "I could do nothing to get the blood stain out of the floorboards. No amount of scrubbing would remove it. We finally had to pull up the soiled portion and replace it with fresh wood. I was shocked to find the very next morning, the stain somehow made its way onto the new flooring!

"My children are frightened. They wake me most every night claiming a man is in the upstairs room where Doctor Galt died."

Years after the Lees left the Galt House, it was torn down, ending future stories of this haunted household. However, there is evidence suggesting the good doctor still remains on the familiar grounds where he lived and worked. When the doctor's house was demolished, townspeople sincerely believed that his spirit simply moved into the neighboring asylum.

Amy Billings, an employee working in the rebuilt Public Hospital, says, "Tourists complain of sudden gusts of wind sweeping through the halls. What's even more strange is sometimes when we arrive in the mornings, the bed in the exhibition room looks as if it's been slept in.

"It's an odd feeling knowing someone is watching you when you can't see them. I've gotten used to it now, and even talk to him when no one else is around."

Cindy Franklin, another Colonial Williamsburg employee, has also experienced strange occurrences in the asylum. "At times, items in the hospital seem to disappear. No matter how long we search, we can never find them. The weird thing about this is later the same day they magically reappear. Sometimes I think our ghost is a practical joker. Maybe he's bored and needs to get into a little mischief. He probably has a good laugh at our expense, watching us trying to find the things he hides."

Perhaps, long after his tragic death, the kind Doctor Galt does occupy the asylum he loved so much in life. His mischievous ghost seems to wander the halls, waiting for an opportunity to play a lighthearted prank. It appears that even though he passed away in 1862, his sense of humor remains intact.

The Public Hospital is located on the western end of Francis Street in Colonial Williamsburg on the block between Henry and Nassau Streets. The hospital is also home to the Dwitt Wallace Gallery. Both the hospital and gallery are open six days a week to the public between the hours of 9:30 a.m. and 5:30 p.m. A pass is needed to tour the building. Call (757) 220-7645 for more information.

The Heroic Spirit of the Coke-Garrett House

The Coke-Garrett House

WHEN VIRGINIA'S CAPITAL was relocated to Richmond in 1780, many prominent families followed the government to its new location. Unable to sell their Williamsburg homes, the former residents deserted them. Soon after the capital moved, the town declined into a sleepy village. As the decades passed, once-elegant buildings burned or collapsed due to neglect. Proud homes, left unpainted and filled with holes, looked like shacks. The grandeur of the city had completely disappeared. Williamsburg was now a quiet, peaceful, and less populated place to live.

The new tranquility of the town was destroyed when Union

soldiers clashed with Confederate troops on and around Williamsburg in 1862. One account reported, "Thousands of wounded men turned the city into a living nightmare. The rainwater in the streets ran red with their blood." Mangled bodies lay all over the beautiful grounds of the former capital city.

The Coke-Garrett House was one of many buildings commandeered into accommodating the seriously injured. Today, this wooden, white-framed dwelling occupies the lot next to the Public Gaol on historic Nicholson Street. In 1755, the land on which it now stands was purchased by John Coke, a local tavern keeper and goldsmith. The original western portion of the home is believed to date from the late 1750s to the mid-1760s.

This stately building, decorated with bright yellow shutters, is actually comprised of several smaller structures. These structures were added or moved to the location in the 1830s. The house combines Greek Revival and colonial architecture. Currently, it is the home of the president of the Colonial Williamsburg Foundation.

When the grounds surrounding the house were excavated in the mid-twentieth century, an abundance of artifacts was found. Gold, silver, jewelry, wine glasses, and pottery offered further proof that a goldsmith's establishment and a tavern once stood on the property. During the Revolutionary War, Patriots who camped on the grounds reportedly damaged the home severely.

The Garrett family acquired the property in 1810. It re-

mained in that family for over a century. Dr. Robert Major
Garrett lived and worked in the spacious home at the time of
the Battle of Williamsburg. His lawn and surgical office soon
filled with unlucky men who fell in the fight. At that time,
there were only fourteen local surgeons in Williamsburg who
could lend aid.

Dr. Garrett worked nobly as he cared for the wounded from
both sides. Although he was a strong Southern sympathizer,
he treated every patient impartially. Dedicated to the soldiers
who desperately needed his help, Dr. Garrett went without
sleep for several nights. The good doctor was not a young man,
and severing limbs was a grueling, fatiguing job. Before col-
lapsing from exhaustion, he did everything possible to ease
the pain of the suffering men.

Amputations were so frequent that the arms and legs of un
fortunate soldiers were piled in the corners of Garrett's surgical office. The appendages of many of the wounded had been
completely shot off in battle. There was no time to constantly
remove the severed limbs, so the piles soon reached as high as
the window sills. One witness wrote, "The building became
so full of blood, people slipped and fell to the floor."

The dead were wrapped in sheets and buried in mass graves.
Amputation pits were eventually dug to bury the dozens of
severed limbs which accumulated each day. With all the trauma
that occurred on the lovely grounds of the Coke-Garrett
House, it is no wonder that visions of Civil War soldiers have
been observed on several occasions.

The presence of one particular Confederate has been noted

throughout the years. This brave man was fatally wounded while attempting to rescue one of his fallen comrades. During the battle, he lingered behind, waiting for an opportunity to make his escape and carry his injured friend to safety. As the Southern soldier stood, balancing his companion on his shoulders, he was shot in the chest by a Union cavalryman.

Somehow, this valiant man found the strength to drag himself and his compatriot to the Coke-Garrett House, where help could be found. His friend survived, but the Southern hero was not as fortunate. He died from his massive injury later the same day.

One might think that all that remains of this courageous man is the memory of his good deed, but this may not be the case. His weary figure has been seen on the Garrett land. Apparently he is seeking treatment for his fatal wound. Since the soldier wears a gray uniform bearing the mark of death on his bloodstained chest, many townspeople believe this vision is the ghost of the selfless soldier.

Martha Ashe, a resident of Nicholson Street, has seen the spirit of the Rebel hero. "I've lived in Colonial Williamsburg for over ten years," Martha says. "The town seems to take on a different atmosphere most every day. There is one thing I've experienced that remains the same, however. It's the vision of a poor Confederate boy lying on the grounds of the Coke-Garrett House, writhing in pain.

"I've seen him on a number of occasions. It doesn't seem fair that a boy with such courage should spend eternity in agony. Every so often when I walk Nicholson Street, I see this young man lying on the ground, beckoning for help."

Martha Ashe is not the only person who has witnessed the spirit of this Southern soldier. Visitors to Williamsburg have observed him as well. One such person is Cindy Lincoln. Her experience took place on a warm spring evening in 1992. Cindy recalled, "I just passed the jail, when I saw a man lying on the ground near the Garrett House. I could see he was bleeding, so I ran towards him to help. When I was about twenty yards from him, I turned to call to my friend Tom. When I turned back, the man was gone. I knew he couldn't have gotten very far in his condition. Tom and I searched the area for quite a while, but we never did find him. Finally, we gave up and went back to our hotel."

No one knows why the spirit of this fallen Confederate remains in Williamsburg. Several people have tried to guide him to a better place, but all attempts have apparently failed. Perhaps he lingers on the grounds of the Coke-Garrett House because he is waiting for help that will never come.

The Coke-Garrett House is located near the intersection of Nicholson Street and Waller Road. The building is not open to the public; however, the home and surgical office are clearly visible from Nicholson Street.

The "Walk-Throughs" of Williamsburg

LIVING IN WILLIAMSBURG, one hears many stories about the past. Just about everyone who lives in this town has had an unusual experience they like to relate to others. While conducting interviews for the "Haunted Williamsburg Tour," I heard several tales about the "walk-throughs" of town. Walk-throughs are spirits of Confederate soldiers who still linger on the streets of Williamsburg. For some unknown reason, they never remain in one place for more than forty-eight hours. Person after person has told me a story about a mysterious, short-term guest they have had.

Although there is no explanation for the brevity of their stay, there is an explanation for what causes these ghostly happenings. On the night of May 3, 1862, the haggard Rebel army left Yorktown and fled through Williamsburg on their way to the safety of Richmond. These troops were literally dropping dead on the streets from starvation. Over 100,000 Federal troops had kept these Confederate soldiers backed against the York River for a solid month. Supplies could not reach the Rebels and foraging for food was impossible. Some soldiers had only a cracker a day to sustain them. Needless to say, by the time they reached Duke of Gloucester Street in the former colonial capital, many were suffering from the severe effects of malnutrition.

Local townspeople believe that apparitions of these starving soldiers are still trying to find their way through the city. Even though there was evidence to back up the strange stories I heard, I found them difficult to believe; that is, until my family experienced a walk-through of our own.

We live in a cottage that stands smack dab on the route that the unfortunate Confederate troops would have taken to Richmond. As we settled in for an uneventful night of watching television one evening, we heard the creaking of our old, noisy rocking chair on the second floor. Our three kitties were in the room with us, so it couldn't have been one of them. Although we quickly ran to find some explanation, we found none. A half hour later, the creaking began again. This time we chose to ignore it.

The next day, another odd occurrence took place. Our freezer door came open, time after time. My mother, Marlene, took a hammer and screwdriver to the door, but she had no success in keeping the door closed. The moment she turned to walk away, the door flew open once again. All day long, the freezer continued to open by itself without explanation.

Our three cats watched nonchalantly as something apparently walked through the house—something we humans could not see. Their eyes followed this manifestation in a synchronized manner throughout the entire day.

As evening fell, the chair began to rock as it had done the night before. We wondered how we could rid ourselves of the uninvited visitor we seemed to be hosting. Luckily, the next morning, no trace of our mysterious guest was found. The bewildering pranks ended as quickly as they had begun.

Although we never witnessed a physical sighting of our mischievous guest's body, I believe it was one of the many walkthroughs of the town. Given the location of our home and the length of time the spirit remained with us, I can find no other explanation. If we hadn't hosted one of our own walkthroughs, no one could have convinced me of their existence. However, after the perplexing two days my family and I experienced, I now contend that they do exist.

Since I experienced my own encounter, I have come across other similar tales. During one "Haunted Williamsburg Tour," one of our patrons shrieked when this story was told. The woman's face turned white as a sheet, and her knees seemed to buckle beneath her. This woman, Margaret Hunter, had a similar experience in one of the smaller hotels on Richmond Road.

"I had gone outside to get some ice," Margaret explained. "When I turned to go back to my room, I saw a man in a Confederate uniform walking silently past me. He didn't seem to notice anything that was going on around him, he just kept walking. I watched in amazement as he simply walked through the wall of the hotel, and vanished!"

On another tour, Joanne Packard, a visitor from Long Island, New York, told of her odd encounter with a Williamsburg walk-through. She stated, "My husband and I had just gone to bed in our hotel room on Richmond Road, when we heard someone rummaging through our suitcases. We lay there for a couple of minutes, too scared to move. Finally, my husband made a mad dash for the light. When he turned it on, there was no one there! The clothes in the suitcases, however, were laying all over the floor!"

Possibly the starving Confederates of Yorktown are still making their way through the ancient streets of Williamsburg, hoping to find their way to Richmond. Although they only stay a short while in each location, townspeople and visitors alike are acutely aware of their presence. While visiting the colonial capital, don't be surprised if you too run into one of the spirits of Williamsburg's past.

Visits from walk-throughs have been experienced up and down Duke of Gloucester Street and Richmond Road. These two roads seem to be the only ones in Williamsburg to host this phenomenon.

Charles Waller Learns a Deadly Lesson

Market Square Tavern

MARKET SQUARE TAVERN has operated as a lodging house since the mid-eighteenth century. While studying law with his mentor, George Wythe, Thomas Jefferson called the tavern his home for two years. He liked this hotel in particular since it was more like a residential lodge than the others in town. In the smaller tavern, only seven or eight people slept in the same room, instead of the nineteen or twenty who shared a room in larger lodges. It may be that Jefferson even had his own room. Considering that the people of the colonial era seldom bathed, the fewer people who were crammed into one room, the better.

In 1749, John Dixon leased the grounds of Market Square Tavern from the city of Williamsburg. He then built a store on these grounds. Later, the building was leased to Thomas Craig, who took in boarders. When Gabriel Maupin took control of the lodging house in 1771, he made several improvements.

The restored tavern, a simple, light-green wooden structure, is a half mile from the Capitol Building. The two front doors and the shutters of the five first-floor windows are painted a contrasting dark green.

When the tavern was renovated in 1931 and 1932, the entire second floor had to be replaced to restore the building to its original appearance. Remodeling during the nineteenth century had all but destroyed the structure's colonial architecture.

Even in its heyday when Thomas Jefferson was a patron, Market Square Tavern couldn't seem to make a profit. While other hotels overflowed with customers, this lodging house barely carved out a living. The reason for its failure was its location. The farther an inn was located from the capitol, the more inconvenient it was for patrons.

Regardless of their size or location, most colonial hotels rented space, not rooms. The only requirement for sharing a room was that you had to wake the person next to you and introduce yourself, so they wouldn't awaken beside a stranger. This was most surely annoying to anyone trying to get a good night's sleep. By the time of the Civil War, Market Square Tavern was operated by the Charles Waller family. Mr. Waller was extremely sympathetic to the Confederate cause.

As the three-year Federal occupation of Williamsburg continued, Confederate raids became a regular occurrence. Rebel guerrillas repeatedly attempted to break the Federal stronghold on the town. Bushwhackers, crawling through the ravines surrounding the town, snuck into the city relentlessly. They killed helpless, wounded Union men in their sickbeds, stripping them naked and stealing their boots. At night, the twenty Yankee patrollers assigned to continuously walk the streets of town were often attacked and murdered. In the morning, people would wake to find the naked bodies of the patrols lying on the muddy ground. Even though the Confederates were trying their best to rid themselves of the enemy's presence, they were never successful.

Under the cover of darkness of the early morning hours of September 9, 1862, Confederate General Henry Wise and a force of eighteen hundred men snuck into Williamsburg. A bloody skirmish ensued. Charles Waller heard the sounds of clashing sabers from his sickbed on the second floor of Market Square Tavern. He threw open the window and shouted, "Kill 'em, kill 'em," to his Southern comrades below. He frantically beat the wall with his cane, trying to spur on his Rebel heroes.

The Federals were forced to retreat from Williamsburg temporarily. Unfortunately for Mr. Waller, the Yankee troops regrouped and retook the town later the same day. That night, after rebuilding their camp on Market Square, the Yanks toasted their victory. After a few rounds, they began to think about Charles Waller and what he had said during the raid. As the liquor flowed and the night progressed, the intoxicated Federals got angrier and angrier.

Suddenly, the soldiers burst through the door of Market Square Tavern and scurried up the stairs to the Wallers' bedroom. The rampaging troops proceeded to destroy everything they could get their hands on, including Charles Waller himself. Trying to escape from the furious Federal soldiers, Mrs. Waller jumped from the second-story landing with her infant in her arms. She and her child survived, but Charles soon died from his injuries.

If Mr. Waller had lived, he might have learned one simple lesson: If you feel the need to cheer your side on, make sure you either have a chance of winning or don't say your remarks loudly enough for the enemy to hear you.

In the decades following Waller's death, people at Market Square Tavern have noticed remnants of the anger that Waller felt for the Union invaders. People staying on the second floor have experienced Mr. Waller's wrath. "During the first five years that I worked here, I received numerous comments from our guests," says Drew Parsons, a clerk at Market Square Tavern. "They spoke of strange tapping sounds disturbing them during the night. Many visitors said the noise seemed to come from outside the wall, but that's impossible because the room is two stories up. Others believed the tapping came from inside the wall itself.

"Then about two years ago, the incidents suddenly stopped. It's been a while since anyone has complained about being awakened in the hotel. Perhaps our resident ghost has settled in for a long sleep. At least, I hope that's the case."

It seems Charles Waller's intense hatred has kept him tied to the site of his violent death. In the future, unsuspecting visitors may once again be stirred from their sleep by inexplicable tapping noises coming from inside the walls of this old colonial lodge. We can only watch and wait.

Market Square Tavern continues to welcome overnight guests. Even today, the country design of the interior continues to be far less formal than other lodges in Williamsburg. Visitors rest in quaint old-time bedrooms, many of which look out onto the lush gardens. It is located on Market Square near the Magazine in the heart of Williamsburg's colonial district. Call (757) 253-2277 for reservations. Rates vary.

Terror at the Greek Revival Baptist Church

Soldiers were buried near the Magazine.

THE GREEK REVIVAL BAPTIST CHURCH was constructed in 1856. An elegant building, which showed the comfortable level of prosperity enjoyed by the town in the antebellum era, it was built on Market Square between Market Square Tavern and the Magazine. The large, regal structure was made of bricks that were painted white. It had marble pillars and a long staircase that flowed onto the street. The church consisted of three stories; the first floor was built slightly below ground level. Towering above most buildings, the structure was a landmark in nineteenth-century Williamsburg.

The church's interior held rich mahogany pews that were filled with enthusiastic worshipers every Sunday morning. Their joyous music could be heard all over town. Freshly cut flowers were placed throughout the sanctuary for Sunday's inspiring services. However, after the Battle of Williamsburg, this atmosphere changed forever.

The Greek Revival was one of the many public buildings which was quickly converted into a makeshift hospital for the men who fell in the nearby fight. The church served as a refuge for the most critically wounded Confederates. Townspeople became first-hand witnesses to the horrors of war as they came to help the injured. A local woman wrote, "Inside the church, the smell of decaying flesh made it difficult to breathe. In the corner of the room was a pile of human arms and legs. A trail of blood ran out the door and into the muddy street."

Shortly after the battle, Northern doctors arrived to lend aid. Although townspeople were terrified that the Federal surgeons would deliberately kill the wounded Southerners, most Northern doctors did their best to save the injured from both sides. At least, all but one. He was called "The Head Devil." No given name has ever been found for this sadistic man. He drank all day and truly enjoyed brutalizing his patients. Victims suffered mutilation under his care. Nevertheless, he was the surgeon in charge of the Greek Revival Baptist Church hospital.

Under his authority, amputations were performed needlessly. Piercing screams were heard throughout town as doctors sawed off limbs. The severed arms and legs were hastily buried on the property surrounding the building.

The death rate at this hospital was unusually high, even for battle conditions. Some soldiers died simply from neglect. Only eighteen out of every sixty Confederates would survive their stay at this church hospital. Over two hundred of the dead were buried in a mass grave beside the Magazine. It is believed their bodies remain there to this very day.

With all this tragedy, it's no wonder spirits seem to linger on the grounds of the former Baptist church. People have reported sightings of wounded and crippled soldiers roaming the darkened empty lot where the Greek Revival once stood. Faint sounds, reminiscent of those heard in a Civil War hospital, can sometimes be heard.

The Harrison family, who lodged at Market Square Tavern in June 1992, had an interesting story to tell about the place where the hospital once stood. At that time, the Harrisons had no idea their window overlooked the site where such agony took place. Mrs. Hannah Harrison admitted, "We saw a young man digging in the ground directly under our window. We couldn't imagine what he was looking for at that time of night. As we watched, we realized he was dressed in a Confederate uniform. We naturally assumed he was an actor who worked on the grounds some time earlier that day. It wasn't long before we noticed he had only one arm. He was desperately pawing at the ground with his only hand.

"In the morning, we asked the clerk what had been going on in Market Square the previous day. She said, 'absolutely nothing.' Later that night, we learned the story of the Greek Revival Baptist Church during the "Haunted Williamsburg Tour." It talks about the mass graves and amputation pits on the property. My son suggested that perhaps the ghost of the dead soldier was scratching at the ground looking for his missing arm."

Although the church hospital where so many died has been gone for decades, it seems the wandering souls of its anguished patients remain. It could be they linger on the former grounds of the Greek Revival Baptist Church, unable to rest until the remnants of their shattered bodies have been found.

The grounds where the Greek Revival Baptist Church once stood are located in the historic section of Williamsburg on Market Square, next to Market Square Tavern. Although the church is gone, the memory of the unfortunate soldiers remains.

The Mysterious Man in Blue

The Williamsburg Theatre

AT THE TIME OF THE CIVIL WAR, the home of the Ware family stood on the present-day site of the Williamsburg Theatre. The plain, square, white clapboard house was a common design in nineteenth-century architecture. Although it was small in size, the kind women of the Ware family transformed their modest dwelling into a refuge for those who lost their own homes during the war.

Out of the goodness of their hearts, Mrs. Elizabeth Ware, a widow of many years, and her daughter volunteered to house a young Confederate who was gravely injured at the Battle of

Williamsburg. Unfortunately, all the care and attention the women gave him proved futile. He died in the home and was placed in the parlor, to await the disposition of his body.

Soon after this soldier's death, Federal troops were sent to search the homes of Williamsburg's citizens for Confederate soldiers. When the Union guard arrived at the Wares' house, he requested to see the Confederates inside. He was led to the covered body lying in the parlor. As he pulled the sheet off the soldier, the guard was shocked to find the mangled remains of his own brother. Although they were from the same household, the brothers had disagreed on the very important issue of states' rights, which led to their choosing different sides in the war.

A source would later write that the Ware women were "inconsolably filled with sorrow" at the sight of this young man sobbing uncontrollably over the dead body. This was just one more grim reminder that the Civil War was truly a war of brother against brother.

After the grief-stricken Federal left Williamsburg to join his fighting comrades at Richmond, he too lost his life to the enemy. It is believed, however, that his despondent spirit has returned to the place where he last saw his Confederate brother.

In the Williamsburg Theatre, which is now located on the former grounds of the old Ware House, people have observed a mysterious man in blue lurking in the shadows. Andrea Carter is one of the people who has witnessed his haunting presence. She recalls, "I could tell he was searching for something important. His face had the look of desperation and despair.

"Since we were in a theatre, I thought he was in costume for a play. I watched him frantically rush from room to room. Finally, he made his way to the last room on the right, at the top of the stairs. I decided to follow him, but when I reached the doorway, he was gone. I was surprised because there was nowhere for him to hide. Later, I was told the story of the grieving Union soldier. If I had known he was a ghost, I never would have followed him!"

Perhaps the man in blue has returned to the grounds of the old Ware House because he is desperate to make peace with his estranged brother. If this is the case, it's unfortunate that he is well over a century too late.

The Williamsburg Theatre is located in the heart of Merchants Square. It is situated in the historic section of Williamsburg on the western end of Duke of Gloucester Street. Today, the theatre shows films. Call (757) 229-1475 for ticket information.

The Noble Gentleman in the Palmer House

The Palmer House

IN THE LATE 1740s, John Palmer, a wealthy lawyer and a bursar for the College of William and Mary, moved into the home occupying the lot closest to the Capitol Building. Alexander Kerr, a goldsmith and jeweler, had built the house in the 1730s. Also on this site, Mr. Kerr built a store where he sold the beautiful jewelry he made.

One night in 1754, the Palmers awoke to an unimaginable fright. Their fine home fell victim to one of the many fires that plagued Williamsburg during the eighteenth century. After the fire, Mr. Palmer replaced his burned-out dwelling with the spacious structure that still stands on the property today.

Mr. Palmer designed his new home to resemble the elegant townhouses favored by London society. It is a sturdy brick building with two full floors. Each floor is two rooms deep, a trait known as "double pile." The first floor contains two unusual diagonal fireplaces, which share a single chimney. The house stands much taller than most of Williamsburg's eighteenth-century homes because it was built on a hill and has a higher roof than normal.

The many holes in the house's outer walls were made by brick masons who used them to secure their scaffolding. The holes were purposely left unplugged when work on the house was completed in case the home ever needed repairs. During the Christmas season, fruit and other decorations were placed inside the holes to add a festive look to the town.

By the 1860s, the Palmer descendants had long since moved on. During the Civil War, the house was owned by William Vest, a local merchant who was the richest man in town. Mr. Vest expanded the home greatly. He doubled the size of the house by building an exact duplicate onto the back section. After the renovation of the town began in the 1930s, this addition was torn down to restore the structure to its condition during John Palmer's time.

In the 1860s, Mr. Vest was deeply troubled by the events of the Civil War. Knowing Williamsburg was vulnerable to enemy attack, the Vests abandoned their property for the safety of Richmond. It was several years before the family returned to the home they left behind.

After its abandonment, the Palmer House became

headquarters for Confederate generals Joseph Johnston and James Longstreet. On May 4, 1862, upon learning that the Union army was heading towards Williamsburg, the generals fled the night before the Battle of Williamsburg. They joined their starving Southern troops en route to the Confederate capital of Richmond.

As his massive army poured into town the next day, Union General George McClellan confiscated the home. He lingered there for one week before reluctantly following his exhausted army to Richmond. McClellan was severely criticized for staying in the comfort of the Palmer House, rather than vigorously pursuing Johnston's retreating troops.

After the battle, townspeople were terrorized by the rampaging enemy troops who quickly descended on the city. All of Williamsburg's men and boys had either been killed, wounded, imprisoned, or simply pushed out of town. The sick, the elderly, the women, and the children were left to the mercy of the Federal army.

The actions and attitudes of some of the local women soon caused tensions to escalate. To show their disapproval of the Federal occupation, the women wore black veils and dresses during the entire enemy occupation. Oozing bitter contempt, the women let the Union invaders know how much they hated them at every opportunity. These feisty ladies did what they could to make the enemy's stay an unpleasant one.

During that time, the Palmer House was home to numerous Federal provost marshals assigned to watch over the city. One of these marshals, Colonel David Campbell, was a much-hated man. He lorded over the citizens of Williamsburg, showing neither mercy nor compassion. In the early morning hours of September 9, 1862, he got what was coming to him. Campbell was taken from his bed at gunpoint by Confederate raiders and promptly delivered to Richmond's Libby Prison. We can be certain his living conditions changed dramatically after that fateful night.

A later Federal provost marshal, Lieutenant Disosway, also resided at the Palmer House. Unlike Colonel Campbell, Lieutenant Disosway was a friend to the heartsick people of Williamsburg. The kind lieutenant did his best to keep Federal soldiers from harming the town and its citizens. Although he was only twenty-four years of age, Disosway carried the responsibilities of a much older man. Many women thought he was a true gentleman. One of them wrote, "His only fault is that he is a Yankee."

One dark evening, some of the troops were drinking heavily. They began to threaten the women passing along the street. Word of this behavior quickly reached the Palmer House. Lieutenant Disosway burst out of the front door and ran to Market Square where the band of drunken offenders was camped.

Outraged, he reprimanded the men for their behavior and ordered them to spend the rest of the night inside their tents. Angered by the orders, one of his own men drew a pistol and shot the young lieutenant where he stood. Shocked, the townspeople rushed the lieutenant's seemingly lifeless body to the Palmer House and laid him out in the parlor to await help. Dr. Robert Major Garrett came to lend aid, but he could do nothing to save the young soldier. Lieutenant Disosway died within two hours of the shooting. Ironically, the Civil War ended shortly thereafter in the spring of 1865.

Yankee troops returned to the north, leaving their destruction behind them. The people of Williamsburg had neither the money nor the slaves to repair or replace the city's lost resources. Williamsburg now experienced a period of extreme poverty. Nevertheless, its citizens were free to rebuild their lives.

The town's fighting men and boys slowly began to return, and the colonial village soon fell back into its pre-war slumber. However, many people believe that one Union officer did not leave with the rest of his comrades. These people think that Lieutenant Disosway continues to occupy the Palmer House.

Near the turn of the century, a family named Tucker lived in the residence. Mrs. Tucker wrote in a journal entry dated June 23, 1896: "We have become aware of a ghostly presence lurking within our home. Late last evening, I was having trouble sleeping, so I went for some water. As I rounded the corner of the parlor, I saw the transparent figure of a man sitting in a chair! He had a pipe in his mouth, and appeared to be dressed in dark clothing with gold trim. He sat crossed legged reading a book. My fear overcame me and I fell to the floor. When I awoke the next morning, I ran to my neighbor, Harriet, to tell her of my experience. She suggested that I research the house to learn of its past. She believes a spirit has made himself comfortable in our home.

"In the archives of the College of William and Mary, I found the story and picture of a man who passed away years earlier in the house. I was shocked to find the man in the picture, and the ghost in my parlor, to be one in the same! I learned his name to be Disosway. I am hoping his spirit will pass on soon. We are frightened by him and fear what he might do."

As time passed, the Tuckers began to feel differently about the apparition dwelling within their walls. In later writings, Mrs. Tucker exhibited a change of heart. On March 2, 1897, she wrote, "As we have seen the ghost of the Federal Lieutenant on several occasions, we are no longer frightened by him. His kind demeanor and gentle smile have put us at ease. We welcome him into our home and family."

The spirit of Lieutenant Disosway seems happy to spend eternity in the Palmer House, although he has not made a recent appearance. One day soon, he may again make his presence known in the home where his life ended so nobly and tragically.

The Palmer House is located next to the Capitol Building on the eastern end of Duke of Gloucester Street. Although it is not open to the public, it can easily be seen from the road. This building, as well as many others, is currently the home of Colonial Williamsburg employees.

The Relentless Raider of the Robert Carter House

The Robert Carter House

THE ROBERT CARTER HOUSE is known for its illustrious past. The house was probably built in the 1740s, although the original owner is not known. In 1751, the Virginia colony purchased the house to accommodate Governor Robert Dinwiddie while the palace underwent renovations. In 1753, Robert Carter Nicholas took possession of the two-story, white-framed house. As a member of the House of Burgesses and treasurer of the colony, Nicholas was an important man in Virginia.

In 1761, the property was deeded to Robert Carter III. The

house bears Carter's name today. He too was an influential man. He owned hundreds of acres and a grand plantation estate called Nomini Hall. When he arrived at his Williamsburg home, he was accompanied by his wife and eleven children. As the years went by, an additional six children were born to the couple. Because of the increasing number of children, the family was forced to return to Nomini Hall, which was a considerably larger house.

In colonial times, the Robert Carter House was known for one of its interesting characteristics—its unusually long, covered veranda. Here, guests, overheated from dancing the minuet, could rest and get a breath of fresh air. The house faced the Palace Green, attesting to the affluence of its original unidentified owner. Today, the colonial veranda connects the Carter House with the McKenzie Apothecary.

In colonial and antebellum times, the ravines and lush pastureland behind the home were left to grow wild. The elegant building itself engulfed an enormous lot just west of the Governor's Palace. During twentieth-century archaeological studies, the researchers found that the house had been remodeled several times throughout the years. During the house's restoration, many "modern" improvements were torn down to return the house to its appearance during colonial times.

In the mid-nineteenth century, Robert Saunders owned the Carter House. Saunders was president of the College of William and Mary and the mayor of Williamsburg for many years. Descended from one of the wealthiest families in Virginia, Saunders owned a large number of slaves and the entire block on which his home stood. Since Mrs. Saunders was the daughter of Governor John Page, she inherited a valuable library of rare historical books and documents, which she kept in her Williamsburg home.

While the unsuspecting Saunders family was eating dinner on the afternoon of May 4, 1862, the retreating Confederate army made its way from Yorktown down the muddy streets of Williamsburg. Hearing that the Union army was pursuing the Southern troops, the frightened family joined one-fourth of Williamsburg's population in fleeing the town. Those who fled the town in haste left their homes empty and unguarded. Some left all of their belongings, including their clothes in the closet and even their dinners on the table.

On the day following the battle, Union soldiers plundered the Carter House. They stole all of its priceless, irreplaceable treasures. They ransacked the house from cellar to attic. The interior of the house lay in ruin. It was littered with mangled antique furniture and destroyed books, papers, and historical documents. Surprisingly, even some of the Saunders's friends and neighbors entered the home after the rampaging troops left and took anything they could find. Many of the recently deserted houses were looted by Williamsburg's own trusted citizens.

Major Wheeling, a Federal provost marshal, later took up residence in the empty Carter House. Late one summer evening, Confederate guerrillas crept through the ravines behind the home and surrounded it. Filled with panic, Major Wheeling fired his pistol blindly into the night. Since it was too dark to see his targets, Wheeling could only hope his shots were having some effect. Apparently they were. From out of the blackness, the young major heard a man's agonizing cries.

After witnessing the death of their comrade, the Confederate raiders fled the scene, leaving the body of their fallen friend behind. They realized the flurry of gunfire would be heard by Federal guards, so Wheeling would soon have reinforcements. The Union officer was lucky to escape unharmed on this occasion. However, from that time forward, all the federal marshals made the Palmer House their home during their stay in Williamsburg. Located in a more populated section of town, the Palmer House was easier to secure.

Through the years, the ghost of the murdered Rebel has made several appearances. Witnesses have seen a man's silhouette, outlined by moonlight, running through the backyard ravines of the Carter House. Alan Packwood, a former resident of the home in the late 1960s, says he has observed the soldier on many occasions.

"During the time I lived in the Carter House, I must have seen him at least a dozen times," Alan said. "The first time, I was lying awake in bed, when I heard the sound of crackling twigs coming from the back of the house. I jumped up and ran to the window. It was then that I saw someone running from tree to tree. I couldn't make out what he was wearing, but he was carrying something long, that glistened in the moonlight. Whatever it was appeared to be made of gold or silver. I was so shaken by this, I didn't sleep for the rest of the night!

"The next day, I did a little investigating. After a long search, I came across the story of a Confederate soldier who had been shot in the chest behind the Carter House. The article describing his death said he was found with a silver saber clutched tightly in his left hand. I was astonished! This proved to me, it was the spirit of this man I had seen the night before. After that, it seemed I saw him quite a lot. Even though I wasn't happy having a ghost run through my backyard, I was relieved he wasn't looking for me."

It seems the spirit of the dedicated soldier continues his raids on the grounds where he lost his life. It may be he is unwilling to retreat until his mission is completed. The relentless raider doesn't seem to realize the Yankee officer he seeks has been dead and buried for over one hundred years.

The Robert Carter House is located in the colonial section of Williamsburg. It faces the Palace Green on the western side of Palace Street. The building now houses the Williamsburg Institute. Although it is currently open for visitors, this status may change in the future. However, its ravines are clearly visible from Prince George Street or the path just left of the Governor's Palace.

A Party Lingers
at Bassett Hall

Bassett Hall

EVEN THOUGH there were bleak times in Williamsburg during the Civil War, love continued to blossom. One unusual story of romance took place at Bassett Hall. This large estate bears the name of Burwell Bassett, who was Martha Washington's nephew. He resided here from 1796 until 1839. The house is believed to have been built for Colonel Philip Johnson, who owned it for fifty years prior to his death.

Bassett Hall has housed many occupants throughout the years, but none was more renowned than its last private owners, Mr. and Mrs. John D. Rockefeller, Jr. The Rockefellers purchased the estate and began its renovation in the late 1920s. Unfortunately, it was devastated by fire in the spring of 1930 and had to undergo extensive reconstruction.

The Rockefeller family donated Bassett Hall to Colonial Williamsburg in 1979. It still remains furnished in the style of the 1930s, just the way Abby Rockefeller left it. The two-story, white-framed home is decorated in an eclectic blend of American, Oriental, and European styles. Folk art covers the walls, and crafts from the eighteenth and nineteenth centuries line the shelves. Mrs. Rockefeller's love of naive, primitive art is evident throughout Bassett Hall.

The grounds surrounding the home consist of lush gardens which bloom in the spring and autumn. Several outbuildings are set upon the 585 acres of rolling hills. The grounds have numerous paths, but visitors need a ticket to visit the premises. The long, tree-lined drive is truly awe inspiring. Nature abounds. Guests watch woodland creatures scurrying about on the perfectly manicured lawn. A little-known graveyard, containing the remains of colonial families, is nestled inconspicuously among the trees.

At the time of the Civil War, Bassett Hall was home to the Durfey family. During the Battle of Williamsburg, a twenty-three-year-old Confederate named John Lea was injured and taken to the Durfey residence to recuperate. Their young daughter, Margaret, tended his wounds. The patient and his nurse soon fell in love and made plans to marry.

The flamboyant Captain George Armstrong Custer was among the Federals who fought in the Battle of Williamsburg. In spite of their obvious differences, Custer and Lea had been close friends since they had been classmates at West Point. When the captain received news of Lea's injuries, he rushed to Bassett Hall. Happily, with Margaret's help and the support of his best friend, John recovered quickly.

On Friday, May 23, 1862, the couple married with Captain Custer acting as John's best man. The two young officers, standing together in their opposing uniforms, made quite an extraordinary sight.

The wedding turned out to be a gala affair. After the ceremony, the happy group partied well into the wee hours of the morning. A grand time was had by all. The outspoken Custer remarked that the women of Williamsburg were the most beautiful he had ever seen. Enjoying himself immensely, he stayed as a guest of the enemy for several days until he was called back to duty.

In a window on the ground floor of Basset Hall, there is an inscription which was etched to commemorate the festive occasion. However, this may not be the only reminder of that memorable day. Tom Abernathy, a Colonial Williamsburg employee, believes the nineteenth-century party continues on the grounds of Basset Hall.

"On a warm spring evening about two years ago, I heard the faint sounds of music and laughter," Tom explains. "I'm a custodian here, and it's my job to stay after all the visitors have gone so I can clean up the grounds. I was picking up trash in the backyard, when I heard muffled conversations coming from the front of the estate. It sounded like a lot of people had gathered for a party. I didn't want to intrude, so I continued to work towards the back of the house.

"About an hour later, I looked at my watch and saw that it

was time to go. The sounds of the party were still going strong. I walked around to the front of the building fully expecting to see a lot of people. Instead, there was nothing!"

Tina Spellings, another worker at the hall, had an experience that was not as subtle as Tom's. Her story was unusual indeed. Tina said, "I was cleaning the upstairs windows in Bassett Hall when I saw a group gathered on the front lawn. The women were dressed in beautiful, long gowns with their hair fixed on top of their heads. The men wore uniforms of different colors that had a lot of decorations on them. It certainly looked like they were having a wonderful time. Couples danced in circles while others watched. Many had some sort of drink in their hands. There was a woman dressed in an elegant old-fashioned wedding gown that dragged the ground. She was dancing with a handsome young man.

"I rushed downstairs to get a better look. When I opened the front door, the lawn was empty! To this day, I can't explain what I saw that evening. All I know is there was a party going on one minute, then a moment later, it was gone."

It seems the Civil War festivities continue on the grounds of Bassett Hall. Since tragedy often lingers on the land, it's comforting to think that happy events may remain as well.

Bassett Hall is located at the eastern end of Francis Street in Colonial Williamsburg. It is open to the public from 9:30 a.m. until 5:30 p.m. It is closed one day a week, so check with Bassett Hall before visiting. A pass is needed to tour the house and grounds. A self-guided tour, with the use of a cassette, is available at no extra charge. Call (757) 220-7645 for more information.

Escape From the President's House

The President's House

THE COLLEGE OF WILLIAM AND MARY, the second oldest university in the United States, is rich in history. During the colonial period, some of the colony's greatest men, including Thomas Jefferson, were students here. Largely because of the persuasive efforts of Reverend James Blair, a charter to establish a school was granted by King William and Queen Mary in 1693. Reverend Blair argued that an Anglican school was needed to teach young men the Christian faith, manners, and good lettering.

In 1695, construction began on the school's main building, the Wren Building. The Wren Building takes its name from the English architect, Sir Christopher Wren, because it was once believed that Wren designed the building. From 1700 to 1704, the House of Burgesses met in this structure, while the capitol was under construction. The legislators met here again from 1747 to 1754, while the capitol was rebuilt after a devastating blaze. During the Revolutionary War, it was converted into a makeshift hospital for French soldiers. In 1812, the Wren Building was used as a barracks for militiamen.

The building was severely damaged by fires in 1705, 1859, and 1862. Following each blaze, its appearance changed dramatically when the structure was rebuilt. In keeping with the restoration of Williamsburg, the Wren Building now looks as it did in the early to mid-nineteenth century. Classes are held in this massive three-and-a-half-story brick structure to this very day.

Two flanking buildings were added to the college in the early eighteenth century. In 1723, The Brafferton was constructed to house and educate Native-American boys. A chapel, where several colonial leaders lay buried, was added to the Wren Building in 1732. The beloved Governor Botetourt and Sir John Randolph and his sons, Peyton and John, are entombed beneath the floor.

In 1733, the President's House, which would serve as living quarters for all of the college's presidents except one, was completed. The first occupant of this impressive, three-story brick building was none other than the Reverend James Blair. Visitors who have graced its halls include George Washington, Thomas Jefferson, and Dwight Eisenhower. During the Revolutionary War, the building was commandeered by Lord Cornwallis, who had a habit of dwelling in the better homes of the towns he invaded.

At the beginning of the Civil War, the college was taken over by local Confederates who used it as a hospital and storage facility. After the Battle of Williamsburg, the college's buildings, steps, and lawn overflowed with the wounded from both sides while they awaited treatment. The lush green grounds soon turned red with blood.

After this battle, Union forces used the President's House to hold Southern soldiers captured during the fight. The defeated Confederates held captive in the President's House were surely consumed with hopelessness as they awaited transportation to nearby jails. It's fairly safe to assume the architect of this fine building never imagined that it would be used as a prison.

During the Federal occupation, a fortress, which cut off the two major roads entering the town, was built around the college. This palisade effectively held the townspeople captive within their own city. The white population was not permitted to leave, while the blacks were allowed to come and go as they pleased. Suddenly, Williamsburg was in the midst of an ironic turn of events. Whites were prisoners, and blacks were free.

One solemn night in 1862, drunken Federal soldiers, who insisted that Southern sharpshooters were hiding in the Wren Building during a Confederate raid, burned the structure in retaliation. Townspeople were prevented from putting out the blaze by soldiers who held them at bay with drawn sabers. The citizens watched helplessly as their beloved Wren Building went up in flames. One witness observed, "The fire dancing against the twilight sky was a spectacular sight." Miraculously, the building's outer walls remained, but the contents of the building were completely destroyed.

Years after the war ended, the college was rebuilt. Nevertheless, Williamsburg did not recovered financially until restoration work began in the late 1920s. Happily, this magnificent city has come full circle to the grandeur and prosperity of the eighteenth century. Now, the Wren Building and President's House are in picture-perfect condition. No one would suspect that tragedy played such a large part in their histories.

Some accounts record strange occurrences in these buildings. One account observed, "In the President's House, windows open by themselves and doors slam shut. An eery feeling looms in the air." Townspeople sincerely believe the building "contains tortured souls from the past." Many have given opinions about who these souls might be. The popular consensus is that these lingering spirits are from the colonial period. Others believe it is the ghost of an unhappy bride. Perhaps neither of these theories is correct. There may be yet another explanation.

It's a distinct possibility that the ominous apparitions within the President's House are those of wounded Confederate prisoners who are trying to make their escape. It could be they continue in their struggle to get away from the building that has held them captive since May of 1862.

The College of William and Mary is situated at the far western end of Duke of Gloucester Street in Colonial Williamsburg. It lies between Jamestown and Richmond Roads. The Wren Building faces Duke of Gloucester Street and the President's House is to its right.

The Wren Building is open to the public at no charge. The President's House is not open to visitors, but it can be viewed up close while walking the campus. Since visiting times vary, call (757) 221-4000 for information.

Yorktown

Long before Captain John Smith landed at Jamestown in 1607, seafaring people had already discovered the natural port at Yorktown. For example, a small group of Spanish Jesuits established a mission on the York River in September 1570. Unfortunately, they were all massacred by local Indians six months later. In spite of its early seventeenth-century settlement, the town was not officially chartered until 1691.

Some of the newly arriving settlers did not come to Yorktown voluntarily. Some who were convicted of crimes in England were given the alternative of coming to Virginia as a servant or laborer rather than serving time in prison. This was a way for the Mother Country to dispose of unwanted elements in society.

There were also people without criminal records who wanted to come to America but could not afford the passage. Although England had been an agricultural economy for centuries, the number of farms was decreasing. Enclosure of the farmlands led to larger, but fewer farms. The loss of farmland increased the number of farmers and their workers facing unemployment. Many of these people opted to exchange seven years of servitude for the cost of passage to America. The worker would become an indentured servant to the person who paid for their passage until the seven years were up or their debt was paid.

These desperate men and women were willing to give up their freedom for several years in exchange for the riches the American colonies promised. Indentured servitude offered food, clothing, and lodging. Sometimes, indentured servants who survived their indenture also received land. Since many were already poor and homeless in England, they were willing to go anywhere for a chance at a better life.

Still others came to Yorktown on their own because of the possibility that they could own property in the new land. Land was in short supply in England, and the land that was available had exorbitant price tags. These brave settlers realized that the chance of losing their lives to Indians, disease, or starvation was great, but if they survived they could obtain property cheaply.

Once they purchased land, the new landowners were required to build a dwelling on the property within one year or forfeit their title. A surprising number of Yorktown's property owners lost their deeds because of their failure to comply with this law. They would later regret their lack of initiative because land values increased greatly with time.

The Kiskiack Indians did what they could to discourage colonization. They were often hostile. When they attacked, they showed no mercy to the colonial families. It was not uncommon for the neighboring Indians to swoop down on unsuspecting townships and wipe out all the people, livestock, and even the family pets. To try to overcome this impediment to colonization, the royal governor promised an extra twenty-five acres of land to any property owner who survived his first year in Yorktown.

Despite these dangers, the fact that Yorktown was located on the York River's naturally deep channel made the town an important port by the mid-eighteenth century. The tremendous increase in trade with England turned the small port into a thriving community. The shoreline was soon littered with dozens of crude buildings constructed to accommodate the heavy flow of merchandise, vessels, and sailors that landed on the banks of Yorktown. Warehouses, taverns, and shops cluttered the waterfront. Slaves and other goods were sold straight off the vessels that brought them across the sea.

In the 1770s, the colonists' resentment of England's taxation policies reached a feverish pitch. The tension between the colonists and the English led to the American Revolution. In the fall of 1781, American and French troops collided with English and German soldiers at Yorktown in the last great battle of the Revolutionary War. From that moment on, everything in America changed. The fate of Yorktown changed as well. Already in decline by 1776, the ravages of the war and the lack of commerce with England turned the formerly bustling port into a shadow of its former self.

In the mid-1860s, Yorktown was once again involved in a war that took its toll on the tiny community. During the Civil War, almost half of the township was destroyed by an accidental explosion set off by the Union army. It took decades for the borough to recover from this devastating blast.

Today, thousands of history lovers stroll the ancient streets of Yorktown each year. With its growing popularity as a tourist attraction, the steadfast village seems to have fully recovered from its turbulent past. Because of its importance as a Revolutionary War site, people will always associate Yorktown with our country's independence. This association will insure that the small port will forever have an important place in American history.

The best way to reach Colonial Yorktown is to drive twelve miles east of Colonial Williamsburg on the Colonial Parkway. You can also reach Yorktown from Exit 247 off Interstate 64. You can tour the historic homes, battlefields, and take a guided tour for a small fee. For more information, call the visitors center at (757) 898-3400. The visitors center is open every day of the year except Christmas,

Sounds of Terror Emanate from Cornwallis's Cave

Cornwallis's Cave

WHEN THE BEDRAGGLED Continental Army left New York for Virginia in 1781, the American struggle for independence from England seemed hopeless. The Patriots had little food and virtually no money. The French and American soldiers literally felt that they were marching to their deaths. Nevertheless, what these forces accomplished at Yorktown changed the course of history.

The man who was in charge of the English and German forces the Americans and French would meet was Lord

Cornwallis. Cornwallis was confident throughout the Revolutionary War that his army would soon defeat the poorly trained American troops. Cornwallis was a boastful man who believed he could do no wrong. However, he showed poor judgement in choosing Yorktown as his military base.

The Patriot forces surrounded Cornwallis's troops and bombarded them with artillery fire day and night. The constant sound of exploding cannonballs drove many of the soldiers to the point of insanity. Unfortunately, the English were not the only ones suffering. The people of Yorktown witnessed the obliteration of their beloved city and homes. Many of Yorktown's treasured buildings that had stood for well over a century were pummeled to the ground.

When Cornwallis first took control of the city, he chose the Nelson House as his headquarters. Since it was considered the finest home in town, Lord Cornwallis felt he deserved no less. Throughout the war, Cornwallis would select the grandest home in the city he was invading as his residence. His stay at the Nelson House followed this pattern; at least, at first.

As the Continental Army's bombardment continued, the English retreated closer and closer to the river. English troops withdrew from the comfortable homes they had confiscated and fled to the shore of the river. There was a cave on the river bank that had existed since the early days of Yorktown. Citizens fled to the cavern seeking shelter from the shower of cannonballs flying through the air. Legend has it that Lord Cornwallis was one of the cave's frightened occupants. It was said he cowered in the corner for most of the siege. Since that day, people have called this cavern Cornwallis's Cave.

By positioning his army so they would be trapped against the York River, the English leader almost singlehandedly lost the Revolutionary War. Hundreds of English troops were so desperate that they tried to escape by swimming the river's turbulent waters. Without warning, a great squall came forth, which swooped away the frantic English soldiers. Thousands drowned in the river that day, while others met their doom from the never-ending artillery fire. Lord Cornwallis realized that surrender was his only recourse.

After the defeated English Army left Yorktown in October 1781, the town fell silent. Yorktown would never regain what it lost. The once-active port fell into a slumber. Only a few steadfast citizens remained to rebuild their lives.

Since that time, haunting stories of the battle have passed from generation to generation. One such story tells of strange happenings in Cornwallis's Cave.

In the fall of 1953, Dorothy Fuller, a native of Yorktown, had an inexplicable occurrence involving this ominous cavern. Dorothy said, "I've always prided myself in not believing in the supernatural. I scoffed at the outlandish stories being told about Cornwallis's Cave. Then one day, while I was strolling the waterfront, a sudden storm approached. Since the clouds were growing heavier by the minute, I knew it was time to head for home. I quickly stepped up the pace of my walk. As the skies grew darker, I realized the rain would soon be falling, so I decided to wait the storm out in Cornwallis's Cave.

Little did I know that I was in for the surprise of a lifetime!

"I was just a few feet from the entrance, when the sounds of panicked voices stopped me dead in my tracks. I couldn't imagine what was happening. I waited a short while, then got up the nerve to peek inside. No one was there! Although I've been criticized by skeptics, I'm convinced Cornwallis's Cave holds the horrified spirits of the siege of 1781."

It would seem the unfortunate souls of the Revolutionary War may indeed continue to inhabit the ancient cavern. Perhaps the frightened ghost of Lord Cornwallis is among them. It is possible the ghostly stories of this historic cave are simply the workings of overactive imaginations, but if you ask Dorothy Fuller, she will tell you every single word of those tales is true.

Cornwallis's Cave is near the corner of Water and Comte De Grasse Streets in Colonial Yorktown. There is no fee to view the cave, and a recording tells of its use during the Revolutionary War. There are no restrictions on days or hours for touring the site.

A Melancholy Melody Plays on Surrender Field

Surrender Field

IT WAS THE POOR JUDGMENT of English commander Lord Cornwallis that put an end to the English rule in the colonies. On August 2, 1781, his army of redcoats took control of Yorktown to use it as a base of command. Cornwallis had planned to meet up with English ships from New York at this port. Upon hearing of Cornwallis's occupation of the city, General George Washington began secretly moving his men southward from New York to Virginia. The weary Patriots made this long journey on foot.

At the same time, French commander, Comte de Grasse,

set sail for Virginia, arriving at the mouth of the Chesapeake Bay at the end of August. His blockade of the York River prevented reinforcements from coming to the aid of Lord Cornwallis. This, along with the general's ill-fated retreat from town to the riverfront during the Patriot bombardment, led to Cornwallis's downfall. His army could not evacuate Yorktown by land or sea. Trapped without food or ammunition, the English commander ordered the surrender of his troops. The Battle of Yorktown was a much-needed victory for the Patriots and a devastating blow to Lord Cornwallis's fighting men.

The terms of surrender that were signed at the Moore House on October 19, 1781, required a formal surrender of arms by the English and German armies. On the day of the formal surrender, thousands of American and French soldiers lined the "splendid field" for almost a mile, awaiting the arrival of the enemy. The victors were elated. Some cried with joy as the most triumphant day of their lives began to unfold. Their shouts of delight filled the air on that beautiful, sunny day in October. The prevailing troops were not the only ones who turned out for the ceremony. Yorktown's citizens came in droves to witness the adversary's surrender.

The bedraggled foreign forces, showing the effects of three weeks of siege, straggled onto the field. Their troop bands played an unhappy melody, "The World Turned Upside Down," as their flags fluttered in the warm breeze. Many of these somber men were also crying, but not from joy. Some wept openly, while others concealed their tears behind their hats and hands.

The hearts of the once-great rival soldiers were filled with sorrow as they threw their muskets at the feet of the Continental Army. A bitter look of hatred shown on their faces as they marched between the rows of opposing forces. One young English soldier commented, "It was the end of the world as we knew it." To them, it would be a day that would linger in their souls forever.

Since that time, the grounds where this momentous event took place have been declared a national park. People from all over the world come to visit the scene where American democracy began. Tourists walk Surrender Field to follow in the footsteps of both hero and enemy alike. A feeling of triumph continues to hover in the air. However, the great sadness of that day has also left its mark in the form of a wistful little tune.

Dale LaBarge, a visitor to Colonial Yorktown, was one of many touring the historic field on a delightfully sunny day in the autumn of 1984. Dale said, "That afternoon, the grounds of Surrender Field overflowed with people. Suddenly, the faint sounds of fifes and drums were heard above the hordes of tourists. I assumed the Park Service was putting on a show for our enjoyment, but I saw no signs of musicians. The song, 'The World Turned Upside Down,' repeated over and over for hours. Some of us knew the melody we were hearing, but many did not. Even though most of us were strangers, we gathered together in hopes of discovering where this music was coming from. Some of us even heard the sounds of cheering and laughter; but I have to admit, I didn't. We never uncovered the source of the song that played continuously that day. Since then, I've learned that hundreds of people experience the same phenomenon each year."

Throughout the years, people from all walks of life stroll the illustrious grounds of Surrender Field. A sense of drama and excitement seems tied to the land. Perhaps the event which took place on this historic ground is so momentous, it remains untouched by the ravages of time.

To reach Surrender Field in Colonial Yorktown, take Moore House Road (Va. 238) to Surrender Road. Continue on this road until you reach the site marker. A recording telling the story of the surrender of Cornwallis's troops plays while visitors view the field. Call (757) 898-3400 for the days and times Surrender Road is open to the public.

The Moore House Grave

John Turner's headstone

ANYONE WHO LIVES in Colonial Yorktown knows the important role the Moore House played in 1781. After the French and American troops cornered the English and German forces at Yorktown, Lord Cornwallis was forced to surrender. The Moore House was chosen as the site for negotiations. Since the house stood out of the path of most of the artillery fire during the siege, it was one of the few homes that was not severely damaged.

On October 17, 1781, English commissioners, Lieutenant

Colonel Thomas Dundas and Major Alexander Ross, met with American and French representatives, Lieutenant Colonel John Laurens and Second Colonel Viscount de Noailies, to discuss the terms of surrender. The representatives argued over the terms for seventy-two hours. On October 19, a peace agreement was signed, which assured the colonies their independence from England.

The historic Moore House is located one mile east of Yorktown on some of the earliest patented land in Virginia. It is nestled on a high, flat plateau, which overlooks the York River. Painted white, the large, two-story, wooden building has two imposing brick chimneys at either end and a gambrel-style roof, which was commonly used on colonial homes. During the Civil War, the structure was severely damaged by Northern troops, but it has long since been repaired.

In the early 1930s, excavators found that three seventeenth-century buildings stood near the house. Although no record of their existence was found, their marl-and-brick foundations remain to this day.

From the time of its original patent in the 1630s until February 20, 1769, the Moore House had numerous owners. In 1769, Augustine Moore a prosperous merchant, purchased the property. It was Augustine and his wife Lucy who owned the house at the time of the great siege.

Though the fierce battle at Yorktown won freedom for the colonists, many soldiers and townspeople paid the ultimate price. Often innocent bystanders became entangled in the fight simply by being in the wrong place at the wrong time.

One such citizen was John Turner, a local merchant. Due to an unlucky twist of fate, Turner was accidentally killed on October 13, 1781, while he viewed the bombardment of the English army. The wounded man was rushed to the nearby Moore House where his loving wife, Clara, did what she could to save him. Unfortunately, Clara did not have the medical knowledge to treat John, so her efforts proved futile. At the young age of thirty, John was snatched from life while waiting for a doctor to arrive.

We are unsure of Mr. Turner's connection to the Moore family, but we do know his body rests on the tranquil grounds of the Moore House. For years his grave was forgotten. Over a century after his tragic death, John Turner's tombstone lay in the basement of the ancient house. No one knows why Turner's grave marker was stored all those years, but it was finally placed over the site where Turner is believed to be buried.

The inscription on the marker reads, "A cruel ball, so sudden to disarm, and tear my tender husband from my arms. How can I grieve too much, what time shall end, my mourning for so good, so kind, a friend." This endearing epitaph is evidence of the pain the grieving wife must have felt. Sadly, Clara never recovered from the loss of her husband and partially blamed herself for his demise. Her death was attributed to overwhelming feelings of sorrow.

For years, people have thought the Moore House harbors a spirit of the past. Some believe it is the bereaved widow of John Turner who roams the house's empty halls. Visitors to the Moore House have seen her sad face suspended in mid-air, peering out of a second-story window. Perhaps she scans the roadways in hope that medical help will arrive soon.

Witnesses have also observed Clara's mournful apparition walking the Moore land. The spirit wanders aimlessly through the open fields. Dawn Truskett, a longtime resident of Colonial Yorktown, is one of these witnesses. "I was taking my nightly walk around the neighborhood about an hour later than usual," Dawn explains. "As I passed the Moore House, I saw a young woman in a long dress standing by the edge of the York River. Her gown and long dark hair were blowing in the breeze. It looked as if she was thinking of jumping into the water. She stood there for quite a while, at least fifteen minutes. I was curious, so I stayed to watch. When she turned, I could see she was crying. She had a handkerchief in her hand, and dabbed her eyes with it every few seconds."

In an excited voice, Dawn continues, "Just then, a light from a passing car shown on her. I couldn't believe what I was seeing! The light passed right through her body and lit up the trees behind her. I can tell you, it didn't take me long to run home. Now, I always make sure there is plenty of daylight before I venture outside for exercise."

Does the spirit of Clara Turner mourn the loss of her beloved husband in death just as she did in life? If you want to find the answer, just wait until dark, and then walk the grounds of the historic Moore House to see for yourself.

To find the Moore House once you have reached Yorktown, turn right onto Moore House Road (Va. 238). Follow Va. 238 for about a mile, then make a left onto Hampton Road. The Moore House will be on your right. The hours and days that you can tour the home vary during the year. Call (757) 898-3400 for information.

The Mud-Soaked Soldiers of Yorktown

The Yorktown battlefields

IN APRIL 1862, President Abraham Lincoln sent General George McClellan and his army of 121,000 Union soldiers to Yorktown, twelve miles east of Williamsburg. They set up camp directly across from the muddy Confederate trenches, which were built to prevent Yankee forces from reaching Richmond.

The Southern soldiers lived in horrible conditions. Due to constant rainfall during their month-long stay, the Rebels ate and slept in the mud. Seeking shelter from the never-ending enemy cannon fire, they took cover in their waterlogged trenches. The Confederates awoke every morning to find wood ticks covering their bodies. Supplies of food and blankets were desperately short.

Northern troops didn't have it any easier. General McClellan put his exhausted men to work, digging ditches and moving heavy artillery around the clock. This seemed an impossible task, since the armored wagons were up to their axles in mud. The Yankee soldiers had little rest as they were forced to sleep on the rain-soaked ground and had no nourishment in their stomachs.

Confederate general John Magruder marched his men in circles day and night, hoping to trick McClellan into believing he had over 100,000 soldiers; in reality, he had only 18,000. Magruder's deception worked. General McClellan sent word to the president demanding 100,000 more men, which he felt were necessary to gain a victory over the Rebels. Enraged at his general's inaction, President Lincoln ordered McClellan to attack immediately. Instead, the Union leader took to his sickbed with a fever, giving 30,000 Southern troops the chance to reinforce their comrades. On the night of May 3, 1862, the Confederates snuck out of camp under the cover of darkness. McClellan insisted he planned to attack the very next day.

Even though no real battle was fought on Yorktown's soil during the Civil War, many suffering soldiers died in the water-soaked trenches. Some starved, while others lost their lives to disease or hypothermia. Ever since those traumatic days, visions of Civil War soldiers have been seen on the peaceful grounds of town.

Betty Guess, a local woman, swears she has seen a Union officer crawling along the outer edges of one of the historic fields. "I watched quietly as he crept from redoubt to redoubt," she said. "I believe he was spying on the enemy. He looked so determined, it was frightening. When I told my sister, Kathy, what I had seen, she seemed relieved. She told me she also had a haunting experience on Yorktown's battlefields. Kathy said that one evening, she saw a man in a Confederate uniform marching on top of one of the mounds. She was happy to learn others have seen the spirits of Civil War soldiers in Yorktown, as well."

Through the years, people have reported seeing "men in blue patrolling the riverfront," and "gray-clad soldiers marching in circles around the colonial battlefields." Perhaps these men are so deeply entrenched in duty, they somehow remain unaware of their own demise. Sadly, these devoted warriors are destined to spend eternity searching for an enemy that no longer exists.

The battlefields are located near the visitors center in Colonial Yorktown. They are situated directly across from the Colonial Parkway entrance. The battlefields are open every day of the year except Christmas. Call (757) 898-3400 for details.

Civil War Spirits Haunt General Nelson's Home

The Nelson House

"SCOTCH TOM" NELSON, a wealthy merchant, was the first member of his influential family to settle in York County. In 1711, he began construction of his imposing, three-story brick home on Main Street in Yorktown. This house is still one of the most impressive buildings in Colonial Yorktown. Here, he and his wife, Margaret, raised their three children—William, Thomas, and Mary. The whole family became quite powerful and enjoyed the life of high society.

After Margaret's death in 1719, Scotch Tom wed a widow named Frances Tucker. Upon her death in 1766, the Nelson home was left to Scotch Tom's grandson, Thomas Nelson, Jr.

Thomas, Jr., born in December 1738, was the eldest of William's five sons. When Thomas, Jr., reached the age of fourteen, he was sent to England for a formal education. He attended Eton and Cambridge before returning to Yorktown in 1761. Thomas Nelson, Jr., and his wife, Lucy Grymes of Brandon, lived happily in the Nelson House where they raised their eleven children. In this home, they entertained influential guests and gave lavish parties for visiting dignitaries on a regular basis. At the young age of twenty-one, Thomas became a burgess representing York County.

As tensions with the British increased, the Nelson family became more and more adamant in their support of the Patriot cause. Although the Nelsons knew their punishment would be severe if the Patriots lost their bid for independence, the family was willing to risk everything for the cause. Not caring what the repercussions might be, the family members donated large sums of money to the fighting Patriots. In July 1776, Thomas Nelson, Jr., was one of seven Virginians who signed the Declaration of Independence.

Because he believed in the fight for freedom with all his heart, Thomas Jr., lost more personal wealth during the Revolutionary War than all of the other family members combined. When he discovered that his friends and neighbors refused to lend financial aid to the Patriot cause, Thomas took out several loans, assuming the complete burden of repayment.

During the war, Nelson was a general of the Virginia militia. As commander of these troops, he reportedly gave the order to fire on his own grand home when he believed Lord

Cornwallis was staying in that location. After the war, Nelson was elected to the Continental Congress. Later, he served as the third governor of the Commonwealth of Virginia.

Despite all of these honors and the ownership of several properties, Nelson died heavily in debt. The general's body rests in the Grace Episcopal Church cemetery, less than a half mile from his former home.

To this day, the Nelson House bears the scars of battle. You can still see numerous holes caused by artillery bombardment. However, the siege of 1781 was not to be the end of the house's military involvement. During the Civil War, the home was again abused by outside forces. It bulged at the seams with the wounded from both the Union and Confederate armies. Painful medical procedures such as amputations, setting limbs, and surgery were done without the benefit of anesthetics. Although the suffering was great, the smell of decaying flesh was worse. The air grew more and more difficult to breath. Because of this, the windows of the Nelson House remained open no matter what the temperature was outside.

With all the trauma that has taken place within the historic home, it is hardly surprising that people have long thought the house was haunted. Writings from the early twentieth century talk of "sudden gusts of wind swooping through the empty hallways." Some accounts say it was not uncommon to "hear men's voices" when alone in the building. While some believe the spirits of the Revolutionary War remain inside the general's former home, others are convinced these restless souls are the ghosts of the Civil War.

During one of my numerous trips to Yorktown, I experienced an unusual occurrence while visiting the Nelson House. Although the third floor remains off limits to tourists, I managed to persuade a park ranger to allow my group to take a peek inside. Surprisingly, when we climbed the tiny staircase, we found the attic was not at all like the rest of the house. It was dirty, musty, and the air seemed filled with an overwhelmingly oppressive feeling that almost choked me.

As we looked across the room to the far left corner, we saw a dark figure staring back at us. The daylight from the window shown through him as if he were made of smoke. Not taking time to observe further details, we ran down the stairs at a blinding speed. Oddly enough, we learned the third floor held the most critically wounded soldiers of the Civil War. Many of them died during agonizing medical procedures.

Two years earlier, Cindy Murphy and four of her friends were walking the grounds of the Nelson House late on Halloween night. The talk of its ghosts had piqued their curiosity. Cindy said, "When we approached the right side of the building, we saw a third-floor window slowly begin to open. We knew no one would still be inside because the house is used as an exhibition building and is locked up tightly after it closes in the afternoon. As we watched in silence, muffled whispers and moans came from the open window above. Moments later, a man's bloody face, peered down at us. He seemed angry and full of hatred. We didn't stop running until we reached the car at the visitors center!"

Needless to say, Cindy and her friends believe the tortured

spirits of the Civil War continue to live out their agonizing deaths on the third floor of the infamous Nelson House. Those who have seen the frightening specter peering out the top-floor window will most surely agree with them.

The Nelson House is located on the corner of Main and Nelson Streets in Colonial Yorktown. The building is open to the public, and park rangers are available to answer questions. Tour times vary with the changing seasons. Call (757) 898-3400 for more information.

Sorrow Engulfs the Grace Episcopal Church

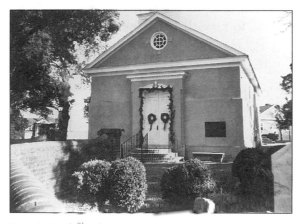

Grace Episcopal Church

BUILT IN 1697, the Grace Episcopal Church is a unique structure made from an oyster-shell substance known as marl. The church witnessed the city's transformation from a thriving port town in the seventeenth century to the living museum it is today. Many of our country's illustrious leaders lay buried in the church's ancient cemetery, including the honorable patriot, Thomas Nelson, Jr.

Grace Episcopal enjoyed good fortune until Lord Cornwallis's English army poured into town during the Revolutionary War. During the autumn of 1781, the English invaders used the building as a storage facility for their gunpowder. During their occupation of the church, the English destroyed its pews, furniture, and windows. To this day, some of Yorktown's older citizens believe that England's crushing defeat was due to the desecration of the church. They feel divine intervention raised the waters of the York River as the English tried to make their escape during the Patriot bombardment of town. Since the English forces were trapped against the raging river, they had no recourse except to swim for their lives. Thousands of terrified soldiers were drowned when they chose to take this desperate act. When their comrades witnessed the demise of the English soldiers who chose to swim the river, the rest were unwilling to attempt the crossing. The English had no choice but to surrender.

In 1814, Yorktown was assaulted by another foreign army. Legend has it that rampaging English militants, angered over their loss of the War of 1812, set the town ablaze. The fire destroyed half the historic city and reduced the Grace Episcopal Church to a charred ruin. No one can be certain if the English were indeed the culprits, since no records can be found to prove their guilt. The only record of the incident states that English ships were seen on the Chesapeake Bay just prior to the fire.

Although the church was rebuilt, it would be damaged once again. General George McClellan's Union soldiers blew up a large section of town in 1863. The Federal troops accidentally ignited their own supply of gunpowder that was stored at the courthouse one block from the church. Although the church was destroyed by this blast, it was later restored and now stands as a shrine to the colonial way of life. The Grace Episcopal Church continues to house parishioners as it has done for three centuries.

Not surprisingly, people believe that the steadfast church contains numerous spirits of the past. In August 1995, Gena Page, a local resident, witnessed one of these haunting events. "I was walking my dog early one morning when I saw a group of colonial mourners gathered around one of the graves," Gena explains. "I could tell they were from another time because of the way they dressed. The women wore black skirts that dragged the ground, and their hats concealed much of their faces. The men wore pants that ended at the knee, with stockings that went from the knee down to their feet. They wore peculiar shoes with buckles, and some had what looked to be capes thrown over their shoulders.

"They bowed their heads in silence as the pastor read from the Holy Scripture. I could see he was reading because his lips were moving, but I couldn't hear a word he said. It was an eery silence. I watched from across the street in full view of the dozen or so mourners. Although they could see me, they didn't seem to care. They were only interested in what was happening in front of them. One woman was so distraught, she fainted. The man standing next to her caught her before she fell to the ground. I felt I was intruding on something sacred, so after a few minutes I left."

Why this religious ceremony lingers is unknown; nevertheless, it has remained for at least two hundred years. We know the story has been around since 1791 because Samuel Hawkins reveals the same unusual story in a journal he kept that year. He too had seen a funeral of the past. Samuel wrote, "As I walked past the old church yesterday morning, I witnessed the burial ceremony of a beloved citizen. I was uncertain of his identity, but the people in attendance were indeed upset over his passing. One of the women beside the grave fell to her knees with grief. I thought it proper to offer my condolences, so I approached the grave site. It was then I witnessed the mournful group, draped in odd black costumes, dissolve into thin air. I now realize that I witnessed a funeral from bygone days."

Another frequently seen ghost is a woman dressed in eighteenth-century clothing who has been observed kneeling in the back of the church. John Carrey described his encounter with this unhappy specter. He said, "I went to the church to do some routine repairs. When I first walked in, I saw a beautiful young woman holding a lifeless child in her arms. She was sobbing uncontrollably. Her long skirt circled the ground around her. I didn't know what to do, so I stepped out for a moment to give her some privacy. When I came back in a minute later, she had vanished. There was no way she could have gotten out without passing me!"

Sadly, this poor woman is but one of many who continue to inhabit the little marl church from the seventeenth century. It seems other despondent souls roam its hallowed grounds as well. People from all walks of life have witnessed mysterious visions during their visits to the Grace Episcopal Church. From colonial churchgoers to mourners draped in black, it seems that past parishioners still come to worship and grieve at their historic church.

Perhaps the families of yesteryear dwell within the walls and grounds of this church, trapped in the moments of their greatest sorrow. It may be they are unwilling to leave their lost loved ones behind and remain determined to stay by their side for all time.

The Grace Episcopal Church is on Church Street, off Main Street, in Colonial Yorktown. The graveyard is open to the public. There is no charge to visit. The church is sometimes open to visitors. Call (757) 898-3261 for information.

A Patriot Dwells in the Woods of Yorktown

Near the site of the 1781 Patriot encampment

THE FLAMBOYANT John Parke Custis, better known as Jacky, was born in 1753. He was one of four children born to Martha Washington and her first husband, Daniel Parke Custis. Jacky was somewhat spoiled and used to getting his way in almost all situations. After his father's death in 1757, Jacky was left a fortune. However, he was not allowed access to his inheritance until he reached the age of twenty-two. In spite of this, he lived in luxury and had everything his heart desired.

Jacky spent most of his time riding horses, attending parties, and living a carefree lifestyle. He was expelled from numerous schools, due to disobedience, mischievousness, and poor grades. Jacky seemed to cause trouble wherever he went.

His stepfather, George Washington, spent a great deal of time making amends for Jacky's misdeeds. Nevertheless, George loved Jacky greatly and thought of him as his own son.

Jacky married early in life and fathered four children. He, his wife Nelly, and their children lived at Mount Vernon with his mother, Martha, while George was off fighting the Revolutionary War. Unfortunately, Jacky could not seem to find his niche in life. He either failed at or quit everything he tried. He just couldn't seem to settle down.

Needless to say, General Washington disapproved of his stepson's poor choices and bad behavior. Knowing how his stepfather felt, Jacky decided to make one grand gesture to gain Washington's respect—he followed the Continental Army to the Yorktown battlefields in the fall of 1781. He volunteered to serve as an aide on George's staff without rank or pay. Jacky's admiration for his stepfather inspired him to be the very best aide possible. His family was shocked by the responsibility Jacky exhibited in his new career.

Because he had lived a self-indulgent and pampered lifestyle, Jacky found the rustic conditions of army life especially difficult. The unhappy but determined Mr. Custis was unaccustomed to the physical and mental trials he now endured. Since the Yorktown area was filled with thousands of soldiers, it seemed as if he were in the midst of an overcrowded city.

As the battles raged, Jacky witnessed horrible sights. Wounded men lay scattered at his feet in the camps and on the blood-soaked fields. He saw his companions die from disease more often than in combat. The lack of effective medication left his fallen comrades in agony. Bloodletting and purging were among the few treatments given, although their results were unsatisfactory. Amputations became commonplace.

Jacky's biggest problem was the constant sound of cannon fire, which never seemed to end. Washington's troops bombarded the enemy day and night, trying to wear down their defenses by never giving them a moment's rest. Unfortunately, this had the same effect on Washington's own men. The abominations of war were beginning to take their toll on Jacky Custis.

Due to an unusually wet autumn, rancid food, lack of sleep, and no sanitation, Jacky fell ill with "camp fever." He was moved from his encampment to a nearby plantation so he could recuperate. It seemed no amount of purging or bloodletting gave relief to this sick young man. Jacky so wanted to please his stepfather, that he tried repeatedly to make his way back to his encampment; however, each attempt failed. His lack of strength rendered him virtually unable to move. Doctors did their best to heal the commander's stepson, but nothing could save him. Although Jacky Custis had finally found his lot in life, success was not meant to be his. He died at the age of twenty-eight.

After the English surrender, the woods of Yorktown fell silent. The heroic Patriots moved on to other duties, leaving the scars of war behind them. The thriving port city of Yorktown never regained what it had lost during the siege. Its hustle and bustle was forever gone. Ships docked elsewhere, leaving the business of commerce and trade a distant memory.

Prominent families moved away, abandoning their once-beloved township.

Now, Yorktown is a living museum. Its beautiful landscape blooms with every new spring. All types of woodland creatures fill its historic forest, as they have done for millions of years. However, in the stillness of night, the voice of a lone soldier sometimes fills the air. He calls out for guidance, desperately searching for the encampment he once inhabited. Sadly, as his nightly excursions continue, no one is there to answer his cries. Legend says it is the spirit of Jacky Custis who roams the ancient grounds of Yorktown.

Paul Brochure, a local hiker, swears he has come face-to-face with Jacky's ghost. Paul says, "Last fall, while I was walking the area where the Patriot encampment used to be, I saw a man dressed in an old-fashioned nightshirt running through the dense underbrush. He was barefoot and his ankles were bleeding heavily. He was shouting something, but I couldn't understand what he was saying. I knelt down so he wouldn't see me.

"I watched as he ran helter-skelter, with no apparent destination in mind. When he ran out of sight, I stood up and began walking again. As I approached the top of the knoll, we almost collided. He came out of nowhere. His skin was so pale, it was almost blue. He had long, dirty blond hair and intense blue eyes. Even with our close encounter, he never took his eyes off the horizon. He ran from hill to hill, scanning the forest below. Finally, he trotted over a hill and out of sight."

Three years earlier, Lauren Duke, a local jogger, also had an encounter with the spirit of the dead Patriot. "I was jogging along Historical Tour Road when I saw a man running about thirty yards away," she said. "I couldn't see him very clearly, but I thought it was strange that he was running in the woods and not on the trail. It was beginning to get dark so I decided not to take any chances. I turned to run in the direction of home. Just then, he jumped out in front of me, not more than twenty feet away. He was dressed in a long white shirt that seemed to glow. Then I noticed he had no shoes! At that moment I knew I had crossed paths with something extraordinary."

It could be that in his zeal to please his stepfather, Jacky Custis remains ready to face battle. Although his body rests elsewhere, Jacky's well-meaning soul may linger on the soil where our country was born. Perhaps in the future, more visitors will come face-to-face with the devoted stepson of George Washington as he runs aimlessly through the forest searching for the long-gone Patriot encampment.

The site of the Patriot encampment is located on Historical Tour Road in Colonial Yorktown. Take Va. 238 (Moore House Road) to Surrender Road, then turn right onto Historical Tour Road. Follow it until you see the site marker. The site of General Washington's headquarters is a short way down the road. To learn when the road is open to the public, call (757) 898-3400.

An Unfortunate Traveler Still Visits the Swan Tavern Stables

The Swan Tavern

THE SWAN TAVERN in historic Yorktown was a stopping-off place for the weary travelers of the eighteenth century. It was known far and wide as the finest tavern and lodging house in the busy "port cittie of Olde York." Consuming fermented spirits was a popular practice during the unruly colonial period. If all the liquor and ale bottles found on the grounds of Yorktown were laid end to end, they would stretch twelve miles—a good sign that the taverns were brimming over with partying patrons most nights of the week.

People looking for a good time visited the Swan on a regular basis. Slave traders also frequented the tavern, spreading gossip and passing along news of the current prices for their human cargo.

Since coins were in short supply, the method of paying for the drinks the customers consumed became a problem. In lieu of change, a dollar bill was torn into eight pieces, so payments could be made for less than a dollar. This is where we get the term "two bits, four bits, six bits, a dollar."

The Swan Tavern was not simply a place to sleep or drink. It also served as a news center. Since people of the colonial era had little opportunity to learn of current events outside their area, they anxiously awaited the arrival of the newspaper carrier. As the carrier approached Yorktown for his monthly visit, he blew a horn to alert the townspeople. By the time he reached the Swan, a huge crowd had gathered to greet him. He would then sell copies of the *London Times* or northern newspapers.

The popular tavern was also the scene of diversions such as plays, fortunetelling, oddity shows, wrestling matches, and lotteries. Notices were posted at the Swan to announce social and political meetings, ferry schedules, and sporting events. The tavern's location, directly across from the courthouse, added to the flurry of activity. Unfortunately, it also was the cause of the tavern's demise.

During the Civil War, the Union Army used Yorktown's antiquated courthouse as a storage facility for their gunpowder. When the gunpowder accidentally ignited in December 1863, an enormous explosion ensued. Many of the glorious buildings from the seventeenth and eighteenth centuries, including the Swan Tavern, its kitchen, stables, and outbuilding, went up in flames in just a few short minutes. Nothing remained of the once-grand inn except its brick foundations. The blast not only destroyed the Swan, but the entire northwest end of town. Today, only two wooden structures from the colonial period exist in Yorktown. Although the Swan Tavern has been rebuilt, along with the outbuildings, currently it hardly projects the image of Yorktown's exciting past. The tavern's present use as an antique shop is a far quieter setting than when the structure was a popular and busy tavern in Old York.

While strolling the tranquil streets today, it's hard to visualize the vastly different societies the town has hosted throughout the last three hundred years. Nevertheless, pieces of its eventful past are still being uncovered to this very day.

One mysterious find was unearthed in 1945. Excavators discovered a forgotten skeleton hidden in a corner of the Swan Tavern stables. The body, found in a doubled-over position, was discovered among the foundation's crumbled remains. With this astounding discovery came a perplexing mystery. Who was this nameless person, and how did he die? Perhaps he was an unfortunate traveler who was robbed and killed by a transient patron of the Swan Tavern.

We may never learn who the victim found at the Swan Tavern stables was. However, if we evaluate other clues, we may find a possible answer to this mystery. Whoever the dead man was, his spirit has apparently lingered in Old York for centuries.

Throughout the colonies, Yorktown was known as the

"roughest cittie in all of Virginia." It was called "the most rugged and untamed township in the New World." Many unsavory characters, such as slave traders and criminals attempting to escape Virginia by boat, came to the port town. Drunken sailors roamed the streets freely. It was a wild, and sometimes unsafe, place to be. Add an abundance of liquor to the equation, and anything could happen.

If a man, such as someone who had recently sold a shipload of goods, was carrying a large sum of cash, his life was in danger. Ruffians would wait for an unsuspecting visitor to emerge from the taverns and then leap from the shadows to rob, or even kill, their victims. If a naive colonist did not heed the innkeepers' warnings of theft, he most certainly became a target.

With this kind of environment, it is not hard to envision that the unidentified body found in the tavern's stables might have been a victim of thieves. Perhaps he was a wealthy tobacco owner or merchant trader, who bought a round of drinks for his inebriated companions. Once he flashed a fistful of cash, the unfortunate traveler had alerted all those around him to his moderate fortune. He may have dressed as a "gentlemen," which sent further signals to the thieves that the prospect of quick money was at hand. Wealthy, well-dressed men of the eighteenth century were known to often carry a significant amount of currency to pay for the goods they were purchasing at the Yorktown waterfront.

In 1877, Thomas Buckner, who had been a Union officer stationed at Yorktown, wrote of an odd spectacle he observed while he followed orders to watch over the "ancient courthouse." Thomas stated, "I saw someone lurking in the shadows of the old Swan Tavern. His identity was concealed by a long velvet cloak. After being discovered, the man fled. Several of my soldiers followed in pursuit. We searched the entire property, but the stranger had simply disappeared."

After the devastating explosion occurred, Thomas and his men went to assess the damage, "which was considerable." He wrote, "We saw the cloaked man walking among the charred ruins of the tavern. This time, to our amazement, he vanished before our eyes!"

Mr. Buckner is but one of many who have witnessed the spirit of the "cloaked man." His testimony further strengthens the theory of the unfortunate traveler, because the spirit dresses the part of a gentleman In the colonial era, velvet cloaks were worn by those of high society. Thomas's writings give us a clue as to the reason for the sad stranger's untimely demise. His obvious prosperity may have made him a target for criminally minded individuals.

Beth Miller, a resident of Colonial Yorktown, claims she saw this mysterious apparition during the spring of 1978. Beth said, "I was taking a walk down Main Street, like I did most every night. It was a beautiful evening. I remember the sunset was glorious. Then I noticed a man in an odd costume peeking around the corner of the Swan Tavern. He was draped in an elaborately decorated velvet cape. We have many costumed interpreters here in the historic area, but I've never seen one so finely dressed.

"However, as I walked further, I began to think this man was up to no good. He looked very suspicious. He was sneaking around the outbuildings and looking in the windows. I decided I was going to find out what he was up to, so I followed him. I believe he saw me, and that's why he ducked behind the corner of the stables. I ran to catch up with him, but he was nowhere in sight. I then went to the visitors center to tell them that one of their employees was peeking into windows. They told me no events had been planned that would require the services of costumed performers. This left me to wonder what I had actually seen."

Perhaps the ghost of the unfortunate traveler remains on the grounds where his body was hidden because he is trying to elude his killer. Or, it may be that the gentleman's spirit simply refuses to leave until justice has been served. We may never be able to learn the identity of this mysterious manifestation, but we can at least develop some plausible theories by examining the subtle clues he left behind.

The Swan Tavern is located on the corner of Main and Ballard Streets in Colonial Yorktown. The structure is directly across from the York County Courthouse. The tavern is now used as a shop and is open to the public. Shop hours vary, depending on the seasons. Call (757) 898-3033 for information.

Misery on Great Valley Road

The Great Valley Road

SINCE THE YORK RIVER has one of the deepest natural channels in the world, it has offered a great place to anchor merchant ships since the early 1600s. For centuries, its harbor also hosted dozens of war vessels, from Comte de Grasse's French fleet to General George McClellan's metal warship in the Civil War.

Because Virginia's settlements in the late-seventeenth century were scattered throughout the colony, it was necessary to select a common port for the immediate area. This led to the creation of Yorktown. Soon, this tiny township grew into a bustling community. On any given day, the York River was crowded as far as the eye could see with ships carrying every type of good imaginable.

Many people of York were getting rich while the town's population grew by leaps and bounds. Magnificent homes were erected, elegant balls were given, and gambling for high stakes became the norm in Yorktown. Public offices were held by the most prominent citizens, many of whom knew nothing of politics.

However, all the people of Yorktown did not accumulate great wealth. Indentured servants, small planters, and, of course, slaves remained at the mercy of the rich.

Slaves arrived at the busy Yorktown harbor by the boatloads. Slavery was nothing new in America. Long before the white man arrived, the Indians had often enslaved their captives. As the wealth of the plantation owners grew, so did the demand for forced labor. In the first quarter of the eighteenth century alone, over 20,000 Negro slaves were brought to Virginia. Most of these slaves passed through the crowded port of Yorktown.

Captives, shackled together with heavy iron chains, were crammed into vessels by the hundreds. Many perished during the long grueling trip across the ocean. Since they were given little food and conditions were unsanitary, slaves who survived the voyage were often sick, weary, and had lost much of their will to live. They knew they had little reason to expect their treatment in America to be any better than the treatment they had received on their voyage.

As the bedraggled slaves were forcefully escorted off the ships, they were greeted by hoards of buyers ready to bid for their services. Many slaves were purchased on the spot. However, some were kept chained together to be sold somewhere other than Yorktown. In either case, all the captives were prodded up the steep hill known as The Great Valley Road to meet whatever transportation awaited them. If the slaves fell, or if their legs simply gave out from under them, they were mercilessly whipped. Many who could not get to their feet were beaten to death.

With all the anguish experienced on The Great Valley Road, it is no wonder people living along the neighboring streets today speak of hearing the sound of chains rattling and whips cracking. An overwhelming feeling of sadness is sometimes felt by townspeople and tourists alike when they travel on this historic road.

One hot summer evening in 1993, Girl Scout Troop 109 from Scranton, Pennsylvania, was touring Colonial Yorktown's Main Street after most sightseers had gone. The area was quiet except for the giggles of the visiting scouts. Their leader, Dana Gilbert, recalls the bizarre events of that night. She says, "The girls were laughing and having a good time. Everything was fine as we began descending The Great Valley Road on our way to the waterfront. Suddenly, one of the girls started sobbing hysterically. Nothing I did or said calmed her. From what I could see, there was no reason for her irrational behavior. Just then, another girl began to cry, then another, then another. I had mass hysteria on my hands!

"At this point, one of the girls took off running towards the waterfront. The others ran after her, all the while sobbing uncontrollably. As they rounded the corner onto Water Street, their crying suddenly stopped. The girls looked at each other with shocked expressions wondering why this peculiar occurrence had taken place. They came to me for answers, but I just didn't have any."

Many of the scouts who experienced this phenomena said they just couldn't help themselves. It seemed as if their minds and feelings were controlled by some unknown force. Marianne Trudell, one eight-year-old girl, stated, "All of a sudden I felt real sad. I don't know why. I was having fun, but then everything changed. It was like I was someone else. I was glad when it was all over. Everything was okay when we got off of that road. I will never go there again!"

Perhaps the agony experienced by the hopeless slaves lives on in the people venturing down The Great Valley Road. Possibly the spirits of the slaves, overwhelmed by feelings of sorrow, are able to possess the minds of impressionable young children as they make their way to the waterfront. Hopefully, one day soon, the land will release the tortured souls that walked this ancient road those many years ago.

The Great Valley Road is off Main Street in Colonial Yorktown. It is directly across from the corner of Nelson and Main Streets. The road is a block in length and ends at Water Street. There is no fee to tour this road. It is open every day of the year.

Haunting Spirits on the Nelson Property

Steps are the only remains of the "other" Nelson house.

WHEN THE ENGLISH AND GERMANS began their occupation of Yorktown in August 1781, they met little resistance from the citizens. Townspeople were forced to sit idly by and watch as the enemy took control of their city, homes, and streets. Many residents hid in their basements, hoping the invading troops would soon leave. They didn't realize things would become far worse before they got better.

While Lord Cornwallis's soldiers were busy looting homes and destroying property, American general George Washington and his men quietly moved into position outside the town.

The Patriots surrounded the enemy and began digging trenches and dragging heavy artillery into place. On October 9, 1781, the American and French troops opened fire on the royal army.

Since the enemy had moved into the homes of the towns-people, the Continental Army was forced to aim their cannons directly towards the center of Yorktown. Many residents, along with the English and German soldiers, died during the bombardments. About half of the city's buildings were destroyed. George Washington and his Army of the Potomac greatly outsmarted the invading English and German leaders at Yorktown. However, the community caught in the middle paid an enormous price.

The Nelson House continues to be the focal point of history in majestic Yorktown. Several cannonballs from the siege remain embedded in its outer brick walls. It was indeed fortunate that the house survived the bombardment of 1781.

However, while gathering information for this book, I talked to Kim Pierce, a park ranger who spoke of another magnificent home which once stood on the lot across from General Nelson's house. This home was not so lucky. "It is rumored to have belonged to a member of the Nelson family," Kim said. "Before the bombardment of town, British troops confiscated and occupied this 'other' Nelson house.

"When the bombardment began, the English houseguests were leisurely playing a game of cards. As legend has it, a cannonball tore through a window, decapitating one of the soldiers. The others were horrified by the sight of the headless body slumped over the table. As they regained their senses, a flurry of artillery fire slammed into the building. The other Nelson house was plummeted to the ground. All the British troops inside met their doom. The only things remaining are the front steps, and possibly, the spirits of the frightened soldiers.

"At times, figures of men dressed in red are seen scurrying about on the grounds where the other Nelson house once stood. It is said, that they dash behind trees and underbrush trying to elude the enemy's fire."

Apparently, the terror these English troops experienced did not end with their demise. Lingering year after year, the soldiers hide from what they fear the most—their deaths. They don't know they really perished over two centuries ago.

The lot where the "other" Nelson house once stood is directly across from the Nelson House on Main Street in Colonial Yorktown. The front steps of the home, which still remain, are visible from the street. There is no fee to tour the property.

The Floating Lady
of the Dudley Diggs House

The Dudley Diggs House

THE DUDLEY DIGGS HOUSE is one of the last two wooden structures from the colonial period remaining in historic Yorktown. All others have been destroyed by fire, artillery bombardment, or the ravages of time. The Diggs House is the finest example of early eighteenth-century architecture that Yorktown has to offer. In the early eighteenth century, wooden homes greatly outnumbered those built of brick, but brick structures withstood the elements far better than those made of wood. It is only by sheer good fortune that the Dudley Diggs House exists today. During the siege of 1781, the home was confiscated and mistreated by British soldiers. It was then bombarded by cannon fire, which left numerous gaping holes. Nevertheless, the house remained standing.

In 1744, at the tender age of sixteen, Dudley Diggs inherited the property from his father, Cole Diggs. Soon after inheriting the house, Diggs married Martha Armistead, and they lived happily until tragedy struck a decade later. Sadly, while giving birth to their second child, Martha lost her life in the same bed in which Dudley had been born. Even though Dudley was devastated by the death of his loving wife, he married Elizabeth Wormley two years later. In time, the couple expanded their family to nine members.

Dudley went on to be a great supporter of the Patriots' cause during the Revolutionary War. He took an active role in persuading his fellow Virginians to unite against repressive English rule. He was also a close personal friend of Patrick Henry. Together, the two men spread the message throughout the colonies that it was time to take up arms against England. After the war, Mr. Diggs served as a delegate for York County for twenty-five years. He died in 1790 at the age of sixty-two.

Although Diggs had a successful career after Martha's death, his thoughts of her never wavered. It was said that he talked to her spirit when the tensions of the times became too much for him to bear. Diggs always believed Martha had never left his side, even in death. He went to his grave convinced that Martha remained in the house they shared together. Perhaps Diggs was correct in this opinion. The ghost of Martha Diggs may indeed dwell within the walls of their once-happy home.

During the renovation of the Diggs House in 1960, Richard Marks, an employee working on the house, recorded his findings. He wrote, "While at work, we heard a woman's sobs coming from the bedroom. Her cries were so sad, they seemed to come from her soul. We ran to the room and found it empty, but a feeling of despair loomed inside. Later that day, we heard the moaning begin again. This time, we were positive someone was in the back bedroom. Instead of charging into the room like we did before, we decided to sneak up to the doorway and quietly peek inside. It was then that we saw a frightening sight! The floating apparition of a woman dressed in a blood-stained nightgown scared us out of our wits! The next day when I returned to work, I learned that John, who had been with me the day before, had quit and wouldn't be back."

Since then, others have reported seeing the hovering ghost of Martha Diggs, holding her arms out as if pleading for help. Her sad spirit remains, suspended over the bed in which her life ended. Perhaps she seeks freedom from the bondage of death by clinging to the last tragic moments of her ill-fated life.

The Dudley Diggs House is on the corner of Main and Comte De Grasse Streets in Colonial Yorktown. This building is not open to the public, but it can be seen from the street.

Jamestown

On a warm day in May 1607, the ships, *Godspeed*, *Susan Constant,* and *Discovery*, landed on the banks of the James River. For two weeks, several of the one hundred and four men who came to Virginia aboard these sailing vessels had searched the land along the river for the perfect location to build their new township. Unfortunately, these gentlemen knew very little about what was needed to erect a successful colony. They couldn't have picked a more inappropriate location.

The land they chose, which was named Jamestown after King James I, was a low-lying peninsula engulfed by marshes. (Today this area is an island, since the land connecting it to a bank of the James River has washed away.) Only one-half of this site was considered "dry land." It proved itself time and time again to be an unhealthy and dangerous place to live. The water was unfit to drink, and the settlers' knowledge about planting and harvesting their crops left much to be desired. During the first few years of the colony's existence, starvation and violence from the neighboring Powhatan Indians all but wiped out the unfortunate settlement. Hundreds of inhabitants died from disease as well. A devastating fire in 1608 all but destroyed the tiny settlement of Jamestown.

The newly arrived colonists, many of whom were "gentlemen," had to clear the land, plant crops, and survive in a harsh wilderness. They had to fight hostile Indians, build their own shelters, and learn to survive in an inhospitable environment. As the years progressed, however, the colonists became seasoned to Virginia's severe winters and sweltering summers. They learned to successfully raise corn and harvest the golden crop of tobacco. It wasn't long before the small colony flourished.

Since Jamestown was the first permanent English settlement in the new world, it was dubbed the capital of Virginia, a position it held until 1699. From 1610–19, martial law was practiced in this colonial village. Then a new form of government emerged. The general assembly was formed in 1619. Here, leaders from neighboring settlements came to Jamestown regularly to discuss the growth and policies of Virginia. Even though Virginia remained an English colony, the governing body at Jamestown was learning to make its own laws, dispense its own punishment, and effectively govern itself. This was the first spark of democracy in the American colonies.

As time passed, the colonists grew unhappy with the royal governor's inability to defend the frontier settlers from hostile Indians. Further, Governor William Berkeley's attempts to diversify the Virginia economy ultimately failed and led to higher taxes, all the while offering no additional protection from Indian raids. Needless to say, the higher taxes were met with intense resistance.

As the result of what some saw as the governor's tyrannical leadership, drastic measures were taken. In the summer of

1676, Nathaniel Bacon and a mob of rebels faced Governor Berkeley with their demands that he take action against their unfriendly Indian neighbors. Although Bacon initially gained some concessions, Berkeley declared him a rebel and began to fight back. In September, Bacon and his followers burned Jamestown to the ground. A month later, Bacon died from a sudden illness. After the death of their leader, the rebellion fizzled. Twenty-three of Bacon's men were later hanged for their participation in the rebellion.

In 1698, the statehouse was again destroyed by fire. This devastating setback was the last straw for the people of Jamestown. The capital was moved five miles away to Williamsburg. It wasn't long before Jamestown was virtually deserted. Eventually, the town ceased to exist at all.

During the American Revolution, the isolated location was used as a place to exchange prisoners. Later during the Civil War, Confederates built several fortifications on Jamestown. They were attempting to prevent federal naval forces from moving up the James River to the Confederate capital of Richmond. A small battle was fought on the land, but it was not between Confederate and Union forces. Two Rebel brigades mistakenly fought each other—each one thinking the other was part of the Union army. The redoubts these misguided soldiers built remain to this very day.

Today, Jamestown is again alive with excitement. In 1997, the site of the original fort's location was discovered. With this discovery came a renewed interest in Jamestown's role in early American history. Hundreds of visitors flood Jamestown

Island every day to see the site where our country first began.

During excavations, the body of a young man was found buried within the palisade. He is believed to be the first English murder victim in America. His body is now on display in the Audrey Noël Hume Center, just one hundred yards from where he was buried for almost four centuries. The musket ball that caused his demise remains lodged in his knee. It's thought he died in 1607 from blood lost as a result of his wound.

With every new discovery unearthed on Jamestown Island comes a strong reminder of the past. The more we learn of our humble beginnings, the closer we feel to the rugged individuals who gave their all in the pursuit of a better life.

Colonial Life Continues on Jamestown Island

The colonial church on Jamestown Island

DURING THE FIRST YEAR of the colony's existence, many settlers who came to Jamestown were from the gentry class of English society. Unfortunately, these pampered men either refused to work or simply didn't possess the skills needed to survive. When he was in charge of the colony, Captain John Smith felt compelled to pass a law stating, "no work, no food." Soon after passing this edict, Smith received a serious burn when the gunpowder pouch he wore on his hip caught fire.

He was forced to return to England to seek proper medical treatment.

Smith's departure came at an inopportune time. Four hundred new colonists had arrived in August, too late to plant new crops. The newcomers were too ill from their journey to help lay in provisions.

When the frigid months of the winter of 1609 began, five hundred souls lived in the Jamestown settlement. In the past, the Indians had provided food to the settlers, but during this grim winter, they did not. (Probably because they wanted to drive out the English.) By the end of that dreadfully cold season, only sixty people survived. Because the settlers feared attack by the neighboring Indians, they did not want to disclose how many settlers had died during the "starving time." Mass graves were dug inside the fort to conceal the number of deaths. During this time of starvation, some of the settlers committed desperate acts. One man even killed and ate his wife. When this murder was discovered, the settler was put to death for his heinous crime.

That spring, the settlers who survived started to abandon the colony. Then supplies and new colonists arrived. With the starving time in the past, the future began to look quite good. Although there would still be bouts of hunger ahead, in time, the settlers acquired the skills needed to provide nourishing food.

What really saved the colony was the introduction of a cash crop, tobacco. The neighboring Indians had introduced Virginia tobacco to the English, but this plant had a harsh, bitter taste. Then John Rolfe blended it with a milder West Indian plant. Suddenly, all of Europe was demanding this sweet-tasting weed.

Tobacco was thought to have a healing quality. Soon everyone was smoking and dipping the miracle plant. Demand for tobacco grew so steadily that all available land in Jamestown was plowed under to grow the cash crop. Ambitious settlers cultivated every inch of ground, all the way up to their doorways.

Despite this prosperity, Jamestown continued to have its problems for the next ninety years. The statehouse burned a number of times. The water proved brackish and unfit to drink. For these reasons, in 1699, Virginia's capital moved to Middle Plantation, which was renamed Williamsburg. Jamestown was left to a sparse group of steadfast settlers. Although much of the activity and grandeur of the settlement diminished in later years, the former capital city lived on as a tiny community. Eventually, Jamestown's population dwindled to two wealthy families, who divided ownership of the land.

Oddly, even though colonial life ended on the island centuries ago, it seems many of the early colonists continue to call Jamestown home. Their restless spirits appear to roam the grounds where they lived and died. Through the years, sightings of former settlers who range from Indians to colonial churchgoers have been observed on numerous occasions. Groups dressed in seventeenth-century clothing wander the quiet island in the late-night hours. Emaciated former inhabitants walk the grounds of the old Jamestown fort.

Connie Smithy, a dedicated park ranger, confided her story of a shocking encounter that she experienced. "It was a beautiful day in October of 1991. At that time, I was the first to arrive in the mornings, so it was my job to open the reception building. On this particular day, as I unlocked the doors, I saw someone scurry into the bookstore. Even though I was frightened, I felt I had to follow.

"I could see this person was hiding behind one of the displays. He was a boy about twelve years old, with dark skin and long black hair. He was dressed in worn buckskins. Suddenly, he made a mad dash for the rear exit. I thought he was going to crash into the locked glass doors, but instead, he simply passed through them and vanished!"

Last year, a tourist from Cleveland, Ohio, had another haunting experience. Sandra Atkins was visiting the island during Jamestown's quiet winter season. She said, "I was sitting in the old church waiting for my family, who had taken a walk along the riverfront. I noticed a person dressed in colonial clothing coming through the entrance of the church tower. I stood up and began walking towards her, but after a few steps, she rudely turned and walked away. I thought this was an unusual way for an employee to act.

"After a while, my family and I went to the reception building to get warm. I told one of the park rangers that the employee's seventeenth-century clothing looked authentic. To my surprise, the ranger said that no costumed performers were working on the island that day!"

Mrs. Atkins sincerely believes she momentarily stepped back in time to see a person from Jamestown's past.

Several other witnesses have also seen the mysterious colonial woman. During the spring of 1995, Andrew Jennings and his wife were visiting Jamestown for the first time. Andrew recalled their bewildering experience. "We were enjoying ourselves to the point of loosing track of time. When we finally noticed how late it was, we realized we were the last ones left on the island. As we walked along the deserted waterfront on our way back to the reception building, we came upon a woman dressed in clothing of another century. She walked silently, with a dazed look on her face. As we passed within a few feet of her, my wife Patty turned to take another look at her dress, only to find no one there! Patty was so unnerved by this experience, when I mention going back to Jamestown Island, she simply refuses to talk about it."

It is possible that answers to the mystery of who these restless spirits could be may soon be discovered. For almost a century, digging was not permitted on the island. Only recently have excavators had access to the landscape. With every new find, we come closer to learning the fascinating tales of early colonial life. Thanks to dedicated archaeologists, we may soon unearth the tantalizing stories that have remained hidden beneath Jamestown's tranquil grounds for almost four hundred years.

Jamestown lies at the western end of the Colonial Parkway. It can also be reached by following Jamestown Road in Williamsburg. Jamestown Road begins at the College of William and Mary and runs about five miles to Jamestown Island. The parkway is by far the more scenic route. A fee is required to tour the island. Jamestown is open to the public from 8:30 a.m. until dusk every day except Christmas. Call (757) 229-1733 for more information.

Angry Lydia Ambler

The Amblers' colonial mansion

DURING JAMESTOWN'S first few years, the newly arrived settlers dwelt mainly within the fort. Eventually, they began to venture outside in search of Virginia's riches. As time passed, a growing number of inhabitants built their homes surrounding the outer edges of the protective palisade. By the mid-1600s, most of the Jamestown peninsula was filled with crude buildings, such as warehouses, taverns, a church, and a statehouse. Some of the immigrants had grown wealthy harvesting the golden weed, tobacco, which flourished in Virginia's nutrient-rich soil.

As the years progressed, the people of Jamestown began to import luxuries from England. Fine cloth, fireplace tiles, and even glass windowpanes were sent from the Mother Country to the shores of the James River. Although several industrious citizens attempted to make these items themselves, their ventures failed.

By the mid-1700s, half a century after the capital was moved from Jamestown to Williamsburg, much of the peninsula was deserted. Its rustic buildings had fallen into ruin. As time passed, Jamestown was divided into two separate sections, which were purchased by two affluent families—the Travises and the Amblers.

The Amblers built their fine home in the style of a southern plantation. A long, flower-lined boardwalk led from the mansion to the James River. The large Ambler family lived a grand but isolated lifestyle. Although loneliness was experienced by everyone in the family, the oldest daughter, Lydia, seemed to be the most affected. Her days were long, and her nights were filled with emptiness.

Shortly after the whispers of revolution began, Lydia met Alexander Maupin, a young soldier who was visiting Jamestown in the hopes of acquiring financial support for the Patriot cause. Soon after Alexander arrived on the island, he wed Lydia in haste in August 1776. At the wedding, Lydia wore a beautiful white, lace-covered gown. Its long train swept down the elegantly decorated boardwalk where the couple was married. As was often the custom of the time, a large dowry was given to the groom. Although Lydia knew Alexander would soon be called to war, she felt in her heart that he was marrying her for love and would return as soon as he could.

After Alexander's departure, Lydia would stand at the edge of the pier day after day, scanning the waterways in hopes of seeing her beloved soldier. Her mind was totally consumed with thoughts of Alexander. She did nothing but await his arrival. For months, Lydia waited without so much as a word. She didn't know if Alexander had been killed in battle or if he simply did not want to return. As time passed, she grew angrier and angrier at the thought of her husband's desertion. Since she felt that someone would have gotten word to her if he had fallen in combat, it was becoming increasingly difficult to believe that he had not deserted her.

Early in 1781, Benedict Arnold and his forces ripped their way through the Virginia peninsula, burning everything in their path. Arnold destroyed the homes and towns of known supporters of the rebel cause. He believed by doing this he was eliminating their financial stability while making them pay for their defiance. Unfortunately, the Amblers' large Georgian mansion was one targeted by Arnold. His soldiers set the home ablaze, leaving the majestic plantation in ruin. For the first time, Lydia's thoughts turned from her missing husband to basic survival.

The family now lived scattered from one relative to another. Happily, after the war was effectively over in the fall of 1781, the Amblers rebuilt their fine home. Again, Lydia's thoughts centered on Alexander Maupin. Waiting for news of him, she would stand for hours on end, gazing out on the sparkling James River. Lydia couldn't seem to shake the feeling that Alexander had married her for her money and had simply abandoned her. Eventually, she could no longer live with the fury that burned inside her, so she took her own life.

During the Civil War, the Ambler mansion was set on fire once again, but it was rebuilt a short time later. Unfortunately, it was abandoned after it burned for the third time in 1895. Today it remains a shell of its past glory. However, the ruins of the once-grand estate may continue to house one of its former occupants.

Catherine Reed, a costumed interpreter at Jamestown Island, is one who believes the spirit of Lydia Ambler still exists. Catherine admitted, "I have seen Lydia's ghost walking the island. One afternoon about three years ago, I stayed late to give a special tour to some visitors from France. Everyone else had gone home except for one other person who was working in the bookstore. After my tour was over, I decided to take a walk to smoke a cigarette. I'd never seen Jamestown after dark, and I thought it might be fun to stay awhile.

"The island has a strange feeling when no one else is on it. It's as if we use it during the day and give it back to the spirits at night. I was sitting on the bench at the Ambler mansion when I felt a presence. Shivers ran down my spine. I was beginning to get nervous, so I decided it was time to go. Just then, I saw a woman emerge from the back of the mansion, moving in the direction of the river. Because she was wearing a gown of the eighteenth century, I thought she was another employee; that is, until I saw her floating in mid-air!"

At this point, Catherine's voice began to quiver as she continued her story. She said, "This person was hovering about two feet off the ground! I thought I could leave without her seeing me, but when I stood up, she turned and faced me. By this time, I was shaking. I was almost too frightened to move. I couldn't believe this was happening! At that moment, she started towards me. She came faster and faster. I could tell she was angry over something. I ran as fast as my legs would carry me, without taking the time to look back. When I finally did, she was gone."

Perhaps the enraged spirit of Lydia Ambler lingers on Jamestown Island still awaiting the arrival of her missing soldier. Is Lydia's ghost keeping watch in desperation, clinging to the hope that some day Alexander will return? If you ask Catherine Reed, the answer to this questions is an emphatic, "YES!"

The bodies of several members of the Ambler family are buried in the graveyard of the old church on Jamestown Island. Most of the graves in this ancient cemetery are not marked, making it impossible to know who is actually buried on the premises. Lydia's body may or may not be buried with the other members of her family, since her marker has never been found.

Carter's Grove

The beautiful grounds of Carter's Grove have hosted a wide array of cultures throughout the centuries. Thousands of years before the Carters' grand mansion was built, Indians called the land home. These Native Americans lived up and down the James River, where an abundance of sea and land animals could be found. Artifacts from this culture, which date back over 8,000 years, have been discovered during archeological digs on the plantation's property.

Early in the eighteenth century, the wealthy Robert "King" Carter purchased the land that now bears his name. Carter had amassed great wealth through his many business ventures. He was a boat builder, a shipper, investor, money lender, and tobacco planter. He became one of the richest men in Virginia. Carter had over 1,000 slaves, owned 300,000 acres of land, and possessed 44 tobacco plantations. His descendants would include two presidents, three signers of the Declaration of Independence, and Confederate general Robert E. Lee.

After Robert Carter's death, the property was left to his daughter, Elizabeth, and her son, Carter Burwell. In 1750, Burwell began construction on the magnificent Georgian mansion which stands on the grounds today. The stately building was designed as a showplace for the gentry class of Virginia society. Carter Burwell's son, Nathaniel, later took control of the property and lived a grand lifestyle similar to his forefathers.

After the Burwell family sold the estate in 1838, later owners allowed it to fall into great disrepair, until it was sold to
Mr. and Mrs. Archibald McCrea in 1928. The McCreas spent
a small fortune transforming the mansion to its former glory.
They threw many grand parties, just as the Carters had done
two centuries earlier. Mrs. McCrea died in 1960, and a
Rockefeller family charitable trust obtained the property in
1964. The lavish estate became part of Colonial Williamsburg
in 1969.

Purely by accident, a seventeenth-century settlement,
known as Martin's Hundred, was discovered on the grounds
of Carter's Grove in the 1970s.

When King Carter purchased the majestic land for Carter's
Grove, there was no sign of the tragedy that had taken place
there over a century earlier. In 1618, an English ship, the *Gift
of God,* crossed the ocean bringing colonists to the shores of
the James River. The vessel with 220 souls aboard endured a
long journey that left many of its passengers sick and discour-
aged. These conditions notwithstanding, these rugged individuals stayed and built their small settlement on a stretch of
partially cleared land six miles south of Jamestown.

The residents of this tiny township optimistically built crude
homes with the intention of permanently settling on the land.
Little did they know that devastating events would soon befall
them.

On March 22, 1622, this brave band of settlers was mercilessly attacked by the neighboring Powhatan Indians. At the

time of the massacre, the population of Martin's Hundred had dwindled to a mere 150 people due to starvation, illness, and exposure to the elements. Approximately one-half of the remaining inhabitants were killed or captured during the attack.

Despite this devastating setback, the community continued. The settlement was soon filled with new settlers and supplies. Unfortunately, the following winter, half of them starved or died from disease. Artifacts discovered on Carter's Grove show no trace of the colony in later years. It is believed the settlement was abandoned by 1700.

Since acquiring the property, Colonial Williamsburg has spared no expense in preserving the mansion and its grounds. The Winthrop Rockefeller Archaeology Museum, which showcases artifacts belonging to the township of Martin's Hundred, was built on the property in 1991. The foundation has also restored the slave quarter, which depicts the day-to-day life of eighteenth-century slaves.

The magnificent estate is a must-see on your visit to Williamsburg. As interpreters tell stories of the past, you'll be transported through several hundred years of history. Gazing over the sparkling James River, you'll almost feel as if you're visiting the seventeenth and eighteenth centuries.

A Slave Named Jim

The slave quarter at Carter's Grove

THROUGHOUT THE YEARS, Williamsburg has taken on many faces. During the exciting colonial era, the town was filled with the privileged, as well as the enslaved. Only two to five percent of Virginia's white population could afford to live as Williamsburg's leading citizens did during that time. Throughout the rest of the colony, people generally lived in one-room dwellings with dirt floors. Slaves, who accounted for about half of the population in the capital city at the time of the American Revolution, lived lifestyles dramatically different from their owners.

A slave's workday, often fourteen hours long, began at sunrise and ended when darkness fell. The work week for many slaves concluded late Saturday night and started again early Monday morning.

Many slaves lived in shacks, while others filled overcrowded outbuildings in the back of their masters' property. Since slave marriages were not considered legal, and owners were free to sell their human property at any time, slave families were often torn apart. If money became tight for the people of the colony, they rented their slaves out, which split up even more slave families. Unfortunately, this happened to two slaves named Jim and Betty and their three children, who lived and worked at Carter's Grove on the James River.

In 1765, Jim's services were rented out to work in the gardens of Williamsburg's most elegant building, the Governor's Palace. He was forced to leave the family he loved so dearly. Although he missed them greatly, Jim found the inner strength to toil tirelessly in the soil from sunup to sundown. He was able to continue on because he knew that late Saturday evening, he would be permitted to leave the grounds to be with his family on Sunday. After a long week's work, Jim walked the eight miles to Carter's Grove, following the curves of the present-day Old Country Road in total darkness.

All during his labor-filled days, Jim could think of nothing but visiting Betty and their children. Each Saturday night the walk was difficult, but it seemed to get easier as he got closer to his loved ones. Jim's excitement grew with every footstep. He didn't mind the journey as long as his beloved family would soon be at his side.

One rainy Saturday night when Jim arrived at Carter's Grove, he found that Betty and the children had been rented out sometime during the week. No one could tell him exactly where they had gone. Jim's heart sank. He wondered how he could go on without his loving brood. From then on, Jim spent every free moment looking for his lost family. Unfortunately, wherever he went no one could or would help him.

Jim died a sad and lonely man, without love to comfort him on cold winter nights. Nevertheless, it seems Jim's obsession with finding his loved ones has remained long after his death. Some Saturday evenings, his tired spirit can still be seen walking the lonely road between Williamsburg and Carter's Grove.

Soon after Carter's Grove was opened to visitors in the 1970s, an employee working on the grounds claimed he came face-to-face with the spirit of Jim. Tom Reynolds said, "I was bringing hay to the horses late one Saturday afternoon after the plantation was closed to visitors. This particular field was next to the Old Country Road leading to Williamsburg. I was thinking how peaceful the evening seemed, when I saw a man walk out of the woods. He looked sad and tired. I felt sorry for him, and I wanted to see if there was anything I could do to help. I figured his car had broken down, and since there weren't any houses or buildings for the entire eight miles of road, he probably would welcome some assistance. I called out to him, but he just kept walking as if he didn't hear me.

"His clothing looked odd and dirty, and his skin was dark and pitted. When he finally noticed me, he turned and slowly walked back towards the woods. I was distracted for just a second, but when I looked up, he was gone. I knew he didn't have time to reach the woods, and there wasn't anywhere for him to hide in the open field.

"About a week later, I overheard one of my coworkers talking about the ghost of a slave who had been seen walking the grounds of the plantation. They said he died of a broken heart. I knew at that moment I had seen the ghost of that poor slave. No one will ever convince me otherwise."

Jim was also seen in the spring of 1997 by Paul Kline and his family from Vancouver, Canada. Paul reported, "We were driving the Old Country Road to Williamsburg from Carter's Grove when we saw a man walking in the middle of the street. I thought he worked at the plantation because his clothing was the same as the actors at the slave quarters. He wouldn't move, so I rolled down my window and called to him. He ignored me. His head was bowed as if he had the weight of the world on his shoulders. He seemed to be oblivious to what was going on around him. I called out one more time and finally got a response. He slowly strolled to the side of the road, never taking his eyes off the ground. As we passed him, I glanced over my shoulder to get one last look at this strange person, but he was nowhere in sight! It was like he was never there to begin with."

Sadly, it seems time has done nothing to heal the heartsick soul of the slave named Jim. Two hundred years have passed, yet he continues to follow the curves of the Old Country Road, convinced that one day he will find his long-lost family.

Carter's Grove is located eight miles southeast of Colonial Williamsburg on Route 60 East. The scenic, one-way Old Country Road which links Carter's Grove with Williamsburg ends just south of the city. This route can only be driven from Carter's Grove to Williamsburg.

The slave quarter at Carter's Grove is located near the reception building. Interpreters describe what a slave's life was like during the eighteenth century. The grounds are closed to the public from January until early March. During the summer season, the grounds are open from 9:00 a.m. until 6:00 p.m. every day except Monday. A pass is needed to tour the property. Call (757) 220-7453 for further information.

Index